PUFFIN BOOKS

POWER and STONE

Alice Leader is an American living in London, where she teaches English and History at the American School. She is passionate about history and about writing, and has combined the two to bring a far-off world to life. *Power and Stone* is her first novel. She is now writing a second book, set in Greece 2,500 years ago.

WITHDRAWN

To Zach

ALICE·LEADER

POWER and STONE

PUFFIN BOOKS

PUFFIN BOOKS

Published by the Penguin Group
Penguin Books Ltd, 80 Strand, London WC2R 0RL, England
Penguin Putnam Inc., 375 Hudson Street, New York, New York 10014, USA
Penguin Books Australia Ltd, 250 Camberwell Road, Camberwell, Victoria 3124, Australia
Penguin Books Canada Ltd, 10 Alcorn Avenue, Toronto, Ontario, Canada M4V 3B2
Penguin Books India (P) Ltd, 11 Community Centre, Panchsheel Park, New Delhi – 110 017, India
Penguin Books (NZ) Ltd, Cnr Rosedale and Airborne Roads, Albany, Auckland, New Zealand
Penguin Books (South Africa) (Pty) Ltd, 24 Sturdee Avenue, Rosebank 2196, South Africa

Penguin Books Ltd, Registered Offices: 80 Strand, London WC2R 0RL, England

www.penguin.com

First published 2003
1

Set in 12/16pt Monotype Garamond
Typeset by Rowland Phototypesetting Ltd, Bury St Edmunds, Suffolk
Made and printed in England by Clays Ltd, St Ives plc

British Library Cataloguing in Publication Data
A CIP catalogue record for this book is available from the British Library

ISBN 0–141–31527–X

CONTENTS

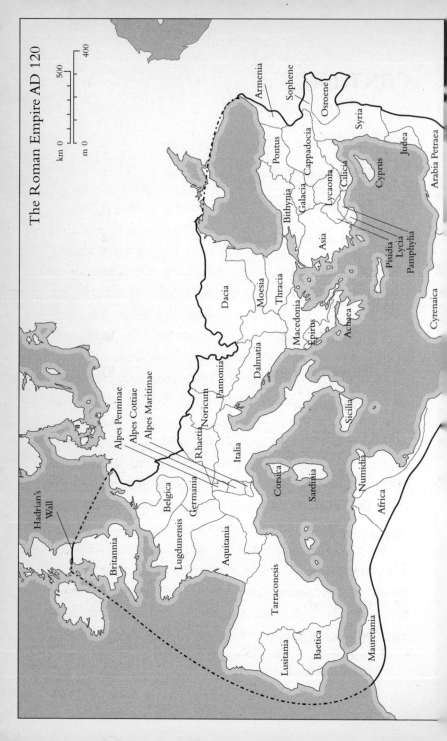

The Roman Empire AD 120

km 0 ... 400
m 0 ... 500

Hadrian's Wall

Britannia
Belgica
Lugdunensis
Germania
Aquitania
Tarraconesis
Lusitania
Baetica
Mauretania

Alpes Penninae
Alpes Cottiae
Alpes Maritimae
Rhaetia
Noricum
Italia
Pannonia
Dacia
Dalmatia
Moesia
Thracia
Macedonia
Epirus
Achaea

Corsica
Sardinia
Sicilia
Africa
Numidia
Cyrenaica

Pontus
Bithynia
Galacia
Cappadocia
Asia
Lycaonia
Cilicia
Pisidia
Lycia
Pamphylia
Cyprus
Syria
Judea
Arabia Petraea

Armenia
Sophene
Osroene

PART ONE

THE BRIGANTE WARRIOR

On top of the tallest hill, a warrior sat beneath a tree, staring out at the huge sky and the landscape below. The forests, the fields, the dotted stone settlements with their snaking stone walls, the streams and rivers, sheep on the hillsides – everything he saw filled him with love. He extended his arms out over the land, as if blessing it or taking in its magic through his fingers.

Stretching across the neck of his land, from sea to sea, lay the Wall. And just in front of the Wall lay the Roman road, east–west, teeming with military activity: mules pulling carts carrying stone, timber, grain; men marching; soldiers on horseback. Out of the corner of his eye, he saw a flicker of movement. Along another Roman road that cut straight up from the south, two mule carts came, accompanied by soldiers on horseback.

He gave a quick shiver. The roll of his muscles rippled through spiralling blue tattoos on his back and chest. But his eyes were absolutely still, enraged. These intersecting stone roads, knotted with stone forts and stone cities, were like a net, tossed over his beautiful, ancient land. He shuddered again, as if shaking something off.

The warrior leaned forward, half rising, to look north over the Wall. There, tribes still fought the legionaries. The Romans had found these lands less easy to subdue, those of the fierce Caledonians, Novantae, Selgovae. The net would not hold. Again he stared hard at the two mule carts with their mounted escort. Yes, he thought. Start with them, there. It was time to seek out the old queen and talk.

With the grace and sure-footedness of a deer, he ran down the hill and dissolved into thin air.

1 NEW WORLD

ALMOST THERE

Telemachus and his mother were hypnotized by the wagon swaying ahead of them, loaded with bags, with slaves perched on every available space. They'd been travelling from Rome for months, since early March, and now it was mid-June. He glanced at his younger brother opposite him and sighed. *Exiled to the ends of the earth with this, my only companion. I wish I were back in Rome.* Claudia heard the sigh and knew what it meant. *Well*, she thought, for the hundredth time, *we're nearly there*.

Meanwhile, facing the opposite way, Marcus lazily swayed with the cart. The ground seemed almost to pull them up over a long stretch of treeless land. The smooth undulations reminded Marcus of the sandy beach at Baiae, near Surrentum, where his family had a summer villa. He remembered digging his toes into the hot sand and imagined how this peat-covered rock would feel to bare feet. Streams were everywhere, gurgling, pooling. Water, mud, peat, rock. The hot sand seemed very far away.

He gazed sleepily at his mother and brother. His mother was the best mother he knew. She and his grandmother had raised them alone. His father had last visited them two years ago and since then had been away administering the new lands of Dacia. Marcus shifted uneasily in his seat, thinking of this father, now commander of Vercovicium; they had travelled half the world to see him. Vercovicium, on the Wall, at the edge of Empire. Marcus had said it so often to himself it had become almost a song. On Hadrian's Wall, at the edge of Empire. He began to fall asleep.

Just before he dropped off, his eyes drifted over the landscape. There they were again, as if out of nowhere: farmers in dark tunics and loose trousers, working the land, some ploughing, with huge oxen pulling their pronged wooden ploughs, some sowing seed. They were quite far away, so he couldn't see them clearly. But they hadn't been there a second ago. This had happened before on the journey north and now he wasn't tired but scared.

'Telemachus, look!' he said, nudging his dozing older brother.

Telemachus was fifteen, much bigger than twelve-year-old Marcus. 'What is it?' he answered irritably, as he looked out of the cart at the rolling green hills and vast blue sky. He scowled to himself. '*What*, Marcus?'

Marcus quickly turned from the fields to his brother's cross face, then back to the fields. They were gone! Nobody was there. Idiot. He hated humiliating himself again before his brother. 'Nothing. I suppose I must have been dreaming.' He cast another quick glance outside; again, nothing.

'Oh, Mother,' the older boy moaned, 'how much longer do we have to put up with this fool? I can't stand him or this cart another minute.' Telemachus stretched his long legs impatiently, nearly kicking his elegant mother.

'Be careful, Telemachus. One would never know you were descended from conquerors. You wouldn't have the patience to cross the Tiber!' She looked at her two handsome sons and enjoyed the evidence of their mixed heritage. They had the lovely dark eyes and hair of Rome from her, but also the lean, muscular build of their Batavian father.

'Claudius conquered this island nearly a hundred years ago,' Telemachus snapped. 'Surely we've been in this cart longer than that.'

Marcus blocked out his brother's complaints. He closed his eyes and listened to the clanking of the noisy chain-mail shirts of their guards, some on muleback surrounding their cart, some riding at the front, outside the cart. After all, he thought, we are important. On our mother's side we are descended from a senator, and, thanks to our father, we are the family of the Prefect. I won't miss Rome anyway – I didn't really have any close friends there.

That made him sad, so he looked over at his mother. He did love her. He gazed at her curls, piled in rows. She always wore her soft, brown hair up like that. He counted five rows of curls, almost like a crown. How did she make her hair do that? Women were very different. As she swayed with the cart, he watched her hair and couldn't keep clear which layer was which. She saw him concentrating and smiled. His eyes dropped down to hers and he felt his whole self curl up in her smile.

Marcus looked out again and stiffened. There was a man, standing stock still, about fifty feet from the road, staring at the cart. The man was half naked, wearing loose woollen trousers and leather boots. His magnificent torso was covered in blue tattoos of swirls and circles, interlacing and symmetrical. His long hair had been soaked in powdered limestone and stood up in peaks all over his head. He had a full, limestone-powdered moustache and wore a huge torc of twisted gold wires around his neck. Each upper arm was adorned with blue tattooed designs outlining his powerful muscles. The stranger's stare turned Marcus cold. He could feel the man's hatred. Behind him, Marcus saw, the farmers had reappeared, watching. When he called to his mother, she told him he must have been dreaming, there were no warriors on the road. But she looked at him with concern.

As the cart moved on, Marcus fell into an uneasy reverie. He knew he had been seeing things the others had not, but what? Spirits? The cart slowed down. Claudia exclaimed, 'Oh, boys. Do look. We are finally here.'

They turned to see the most extraordinary sight. They had to stick their heads out of the cart, craning their necks to look far enough up. Rising before them, and then running as far left and as far right as they could see, was a huge, white wall, overbearing, imposing, with soldiers patrolling along its top, and suddenly at least a hundred were before them, exercising and practising all around their cart.

'Telemachus! Look! Those are auxiliaries from ... from ...'

'From Tungria! That's the Tungrian Cohort, Marcus! They're the *milliaria peditata* – you remember! Their heavy infantry held the line so well at Mons Graupius. Everyone said the legionaries couldn't have done better.'

Marcus hated it when Telemachus treated him like a little boy who didn't know anything, so he showed off his own knowledge. 'Oh, yes? Don't forget the help they got from Father's people. The Batavians were the lighter and swifter ones at that battle.' But Telemachus wasn't listening.

'Look at the armour they're wearing!' What are they throwing for javelins? Telemachus wondered. Those aren't the usual *pila*. Oh, they're throwing *hastati*, because they're auxiliaries from . . . Germania. Only legionaries can throw *pila*, he reminded himself. 'Mother! The auxiliaries are manning the forts now, aren't they? Are the legionaries all gone, now that the Wall is finished?'

'Ho! Slow down.' The noise of the soldiers made it difficult for her to answer her son. 'The Wall isn't entirely finished,' she almost shouted. 'There are still some forts to be completed, and milecastles and turrets. They're almost done, but not quite. Anyway,' she did shout, 'there are three complete legions and several thousand auxiliaries up here still.'

Oh, how Marcus wanted to look like the soldiers. Legionaries may be from Rome or from any of the provinces, but they are citizens of Rome, he recited to himself. And auxiliaries, enlisted from the provinces, hope to be citizens after their twenty-five-year service in the army. Legionaries are much more important. Then he thought about his father, who started his career as an auxiliary. He used to look like those men. Maybe he still did . . . His mind refused to remember clearly. But the man he could remember was very fit, very strong and somehow reserved, quiet, judgemental. Marcus looked ahead nervously.

Telemachus wasn't thinking about their father. He was dreaming of himself as a heroic legionary, powerful, competent, leading the charge against wild, filthy barbarians. He would be decorated for his bravery, crowds in Rome would cheer, the Emperor would beckon to him.

They were now surrounded by the *vicus*, a settlement of little cobbled streets with houses, open-fronted shops and taverns. A bit removed from these buildings they saw bath-houses belching heavy, dark smoke. Stone buildings with shingled or thatched roofs filled their view. There must be over fifty buildings here, Telemachus thought. All pressed together, but with proper streets and drainage, properly covered drains. Where did all these buildings come from? he wondered.

People flowed around the carts, jostling the travellers, calling to each other. The air was filled with smells – of bakeries, butcher's and fishmonger's shops, leather tanneries and fireplaces. The din was bewildering.

Claudia looked out from her side of the cart. Not all the Brigantes were rough, she noticed. Some women, for instance, were well dressed with beautifully woven shawls around their shoulders, their hair neatly braided into complicated, flattering styles. Who were these women? How did they live? Were they really as comfortable as they seemed, mingling with the conquerors, with the tribal soldiers from the continent, their wives, children and kinfolk? How odd the whole scene seemed to her: a lively settlement on the brink of nowhere.

The cart rolled on to the entrance of the fort. Tall double gates opened and in they went, jostled by the uneven cobblestones, jarring against the stone wall of the guardhouse, unsteadily drawn by tired mules. The eyes of the newcomers were filled with more visions of stone. Vercovicium consisted of as many as twenty or even thirty buildings surrounded by a fifteen-foot stone wall. Each side of the fort was broken by a guardhouse with double doors, interrogation area, another set of double doors. The sky itself was dark grey that day, though it was mid-summer.

Mounted soldiers bristling with mail armour, swords, shields and completely enclosed helmets thundered out of the fort. A *cornicen* blew his horn and a clearly irritated centurion barked orders at his assembled auxiliaries, while other soldiers ran by him carrying heavy bags of grain. More men were carrying water and dumping it into two stone cisterns on a rise at the bottom end of the fort. Others of different ranks strolled by, laughing and joking, headed for the bathhouse, Marcus guessed by the sandals they carried dangling over their shoulders. Grain was being loaded or unloaded at the granaries, and carts were being pulled by horses everywhere. After weeks encased in that mule cart, there was too much activity to take in at once. And this was to be his home! This is my father's fort, he thought. This is splendid. He turned with a huge grin to his brother and mother.

They were a sight. In the midst of all this activity, mother and son sat immobile. Elegant, still, composed, their faces mask-like, they commanded attention. Suddenly Marcus remembered his duties as a son of Rome. He too sat to attention. His face lost all expression and became timeless as a statue's. The leader of their military escort drew himself up before them, bowed and led the way to the centre of the fort, to the Praetorium. This was the home of the Prefect and now would be theirs too. They walked straight down the central street of the fort, looking neither left nor right. Marcus was aware of men staring at them, or really at his mother, and his cheeks flushed. Always beautiful, here she was a goddess, outside reality entirely. The men dropped their eyes immediately. The escort took them directly into the house at the entrance hall. The three knew to file into the next room, the waiting room, and sit on the marble bench running along the four walls. The escort bowed again and left them. Moments later he re-appeared, followed by Gaius Decimus Rufinus, commander of Vercovicium, husband and father.

GAIUS DECIMUS RUFINUS

Gaius never disappointed. The boys were mesmerized. Marcus's jaw dropped slightly as he stared. Telemachus's face darkened, so sure already of his own inadequacy. He is more powerful than I remembered, he thought. I will never be able to please this professional soldier. The boys watched their parents. As he crossed the room to greet his wife, Gaius's lithe body moved easily under his decorated steel breastplate. The boys saw their mother's eye catch the flashes of white skin just under the armour at his neck and upper arms as he reached out to embrace her. He pressed her to his chest, and they saw her close her eyes. The boys hadn't seen that look of happiness on her face for two years. Suddenly they both felt calm.

'Two years,' Gaius whispered in her ear. It was good to hold her again. His hands slid down her back, following the curve from her wide shoulders to her small waist.

Although the embrace was embarrassing to watch, the boys were deeply pleased to see their parents together again. Maybe this time it will work better, Telemachus thought. Marcus kept his eyes glued to his mother's face. Then Gaius stepped back suddenly, setting in motion the formalities of the family reunion.

He approached the boys. Telemachus stood stiffly, looking straight ahead. He wanted his father to see how tall he'd grown and how he was ready to receive commands. Marcus quickly glanced at his father and then bowed, looking into the middle distance. Claudia slowly turned to gaze fully into the face of her husband. Keeping a straight back, she bent one knee and descended a few inches, holding her shoulders and head still. The diaphanous folds of her soft linen travelling robe fell prettily in creamy pleats and gentle mounds on to the painted stone floor. Because of the angle at which she held her head, her neck and the hollows beneath her jaw were most noticeable and beautiful. She knew she looked like nothing else for hundreds of miles. There was no conceit in her at all, rather the sure sense of her role as wife of the commander.

Gaius took in his family. First, Telemachus. He tried to remember: fifteen, wasn't he? He saw the boy's stern bearing and dignity and recognized a potential soldier. That this handsome, strong, curly-haired son clearly wanted to be a soldier filled him with pride. Then the familiar wave of guilt swept over his heart as he remembered how long he'd been away from his family in the Dacian campaign. But it couldn't be helped; as one of Trajan's cohort commanders, he was obliged to administer as well as he could the newly conquered Dacia; he had done so well that he had been promoted to command Vercovicium. He had had no choice. Still, the sight of his son trying so hard to impress touched, flattered and shamed Gaius. He vowed to attend now, personally, to his education and career. He had seen thousands of new recruits, yet this was one of his blood.

Telemachus sensed his interest and was relieved.

Gaius turned to look at his second son, the 'spare', good insurance against catastrophe. Twelve years old, yes. He thanked the gods for two such fine boys. He smiled to himself when he saw Marcus steal a glance at him. His younger son, though well formed and athletic-looking, was probably still tied to his mother. Might be one of those reflective sorts, he mused. He saw Marcus already losing interest in the moment and beginning to look around the waiting room at all the people and his new surroundings.

Although Marcus was, indeed, staring at two new people who had just slipped into the room, Telemachus watched carefully as his father turned his attention to Claudia. He looked to see what his father was seeing. She was still beautiful. Her brown curls were swept up. She had large green-hazel eyes and smoothly arched eyebrows, a wide, generous mouth and a sweet smile. Marcus, paying attention again and looking at his mother too, suddenly wished he could just hug her, he loved her so much and was so proud of her. His parents had been married sixteen years but had lived together less than twelve months. The boys watched her face closely. If this reunion worked, they would stay. If it didn't, they would be returning soon to Rome.

They had always known, for all their mother's protestations, that it was usual for a commander of their father's stature to be in the field, away from Rome most of the time. They hadn't liked it that their father had been so often absent. Telemachus had been forced to delay his *toga virilis* ceremony twice, waiting for his father to be available; all of his friends had had theirs, mostly by the time they were twelve. And they both missed the presence of their father in their daily lives. They also felt their mother's loneliness. But they knew, as she did, as their father now did, that it was time for them to present their strengths and weaknesses before him, to see what he could make of them. Vercovicium's Praetorium had just been finished and it was appropriate that the Prefect's family should arrive. That delicate shifting of responsibility for the boys' upbringing had just begun, in the waiting room of the Praetorium, at midsummer in the thirteenth year of the reign of Hadrian.

VERCOVICIUM: FIRST FRIENDS

'Claudia,' Gaius interrupted the boys' thoughts, 'I would like to introduce two people who will help you here at Vercovicium.'

The family and attendants parted, revealing a young woman and an old man standing at the back of the room. She was attractive, slender, a Roman woman of almost thirty, only a few years younger than Claudia. The elderly man, probably a retired soldier, hung back and stood behind the group. Claudia was riveted by the woman. She had not expected to see a Roman woman here. She liked her intelligent look and athletic, poised bearing but could tell she was not a lady of the senatorial class, as Claudia was. She was somehow foreign, not wholly Roman. But how wonderful to have a companion, she thought. At least this is somebody with whom I can talk.

The woman did not look at Claudia directly. She wore her black hair pulled back into a bun, very different from Claudia's helmet of curls. Over a long, tight-fitting, orange-coloured tunic, she wore a loose white linen tunic and, around her shoulders, a delicately woven red shawl which fell to the ground and draped elegantly around her feet. The only aspect of her dress that suggested foreign influence was the garish colour.

'I am amazed,' Claudia cheerfully declared. 'After

travelling for months, I am greeted by a lady from Rome.' Claudia gracefully dipped her head in an abbreviated curtsy. She saw, out of the corner of her eye, that the woman was pleased to be so formally greeted. She glanced swiftly at Gaius.

'Brigit's story is most extraordinary. She is, indeed, a Roman lady.' Gaius smiled, pleased with himself for finding this suitable companion for his wife. 'But her heritage is Brigantian.'

Claudia and the boys looked surprised and interested in this, their first Brigante.

'Her great-grandmother served Queen Cartimandua sixty years ago, and then, with her family and a few other Brigantes, she moved to Rome, when Cartimandua graciously passed her throne to the Empire,' he said, with a broad politician's smile. 'These Brigantes established a little community, intermarrying and passing down clan and tribal traditions. And here is the result! Brigit, born and bred in Rome, nevertheless considers herself a Brigante, and she decided a year ago to come here and live among her clan and tribe. Her family roots are south of here, closer to Eboracum, but she wished to live with her farming cousins near Vercovicium. I suspect that she quite misses our Roman ways, for she has agreed to be your companion here at Vercovicium. Until we lose her to some lucky husband, nothing could please me more!' he concluded with a confident smile.

Surprise hung in the air after he had finished speaking. The boys were intrigued by this unexpected reference to the

15

Brigantes. Telemachus immediately began to imagine himself valiantly leading auxiliaries into battle. Marcus liked the idea of a queen and silently sounded out Car-ti-man-du-a. But Claudia's reaction was the strongest, for she was genuinely relieved to find this woman at Vercovicium. She speaks Latin, she knows Rome, she knows the local ways too! What a superb bit of luck. Her look to Gaius conveying her heartfelt gratitude pleased him very much.

Brigit looked directly at Claudia. Claudia and the boys were a little surprised at her straightforward manner. After all, she was to be the companion of the Prefect's wife, not her social equal. Yet she was so natural and sure of herself they were charmed. 'I have very much missed the Roman ways and am very glad you are here,' she began, 'and if you become interested in Brigantian ways, I would gladly show them to you.'

While maintaining a smooth, serene expression, Claudia pondered Brigit. That an attractive, elegant young woman would choose to leave Rome and live up here in cold Britannia, surrounded by sheep and soldiers, puzzled her, especially since her family roots were to the south. Telemachus, meanwhile, grew very pleased, as he'd just remembered what his teacher in Rome had told him about the northern tribes of Britannia: sometimes they removed the brains from their enemies' heads, rolled them into balls, dried the balls in the sun and then carved faces on the hard surface. These 'brain-balls' they used as weapons, throwing them at new enemies. Besides being good to throw, the balls were supposed to have magical powers, leading to victory over other enemies. Telemachus was pretty sure he'd like to learn more about such customs. Marcus, in contrast, was growing bored with formality and woman-talk.

'I should be very interested to learn something of Brigantian history, Brigit,' Claudia answered. 'All I know of Queen Cartimandua is that she was a friend of Rome. My great-grandfather was in the Senate when your great-grandmother was serving the queen!' Suddenly Claudia felt uneasy, fearing she might have upset Brigit. What had the *optio* told her as they travelled north? The Brigantes, a huge tribe whose ancestral lands covered much of northern Britannia, had retained their independence longer than most 'kingdoms' by forming an alliance with Rome. Then the tribe's anti-Roman king had forced Rome to revoke the alliance and declared war. After defeating the king, Rome conquered the Brigantian lands and built the Wall, forts and roads criss-crossing the territory. Not a happy history for a Brigante. Yet the people here were on the whole friendly with Rome, she'd been told.

And then she understood what had puzzled her about Brigit. She had reversed the pattern. The pattern for conquered peoples was to do their best to gain Roman citizenship and establish a connection with the powers in Rome. She had rejected Rome – and gone to the most distant point in the Empire. Maybe she had inherited lands, which, by Brigantian tradition, women could do. Yet if she had, she hadn't chosen to live on them. And why wasn't she married?

Brigit stood clear-browed and calm. 'I wish I had known

Cartimandua. She was a clever, shrewd ruler, very good at manipulating men, wielding power, and a great admirer of the luxuries of the Roman Empire.' She smiled.

Claudia smiled back. She did not want Brigit as an enemy – there were too few women along the Wall, much less in this fort. 'I look forward to understanding more. Thank you for consenting to be my companion. I am most grateful and relieved.'

'It is I who should be thanking you,' Brigit said quietly, quickly glancing into Claudia's eyes. She hesitated. 'I've taken a liberty on our first day together to invite a boy of our tribe to give your sons a tour. I hope that's all right.'

Claudia looked quickly to Gaius for direction. After all, this was their first day on the Wall. Although the Brigantes had been in alliance with the Romans for over sixty years, other tribes on the Wall were hostile and aggressive. The boys didn't know where they were, where it was safe or whom to trust.

'It's Bran, isn't it, Brigit? He's a fine lad. I know him well.' Gaius lowered his voice and confided, 'His father was killed ten years ago in one of the many skirmishes we had with the Selgovae and Novantae.' The boys grew alert. 'He, along with his tribe –' here Gaius gave Brigit a nod – 'had supported our occupation of Britannia, welcomed us with open arms, as they knew from their trade network with Gaul the benefits of being part of the Empire. It was important to us that the Brigantes were our allies.' The two boys gazed at their impressive, proud father. Gaius continued: 'We built the Wall in part to protect them and the tribes further south from these fierce northern tribes. Bran was only two at the time, his sister only five. Raising two children has been hard on the widow, Modron.'

The family received this information uneasily.

'Anyway, you'll like Bran,' he said, smiling into Marcus's attentive and worried face.

'What are the Selgovae like? Are the Novantae more fierce? Are they still our enemies?'

Marcus peppered him with questions until Gaius looked directly at him and raised an eyebrow. Immediately, Marcus fell silent, but was pleased with this secret communication between himself and his father. Telemachus saw it all and was as jealous as Marcus was flattered.

Gaius now asked, with an almost booming cheerfulness, 'Is Bran here now, Brigit?'

'Yes.' Brigit smiled, taking her turn this time to look reassuringly right into Claudia's eyes. 'I know everyone around here and know this is a good friend to have.' She looked at Gaius for permission. He nodded and she called, 'Bran!'

Into the room came a strong, athletic boy with dark hair and eyes. About twelve years old, he held his head high in a confident but not a conceited way. His demeanour announced to the world that he was used to loving and being loved.

This was the most mischievous, fun-looking person that Marcus had seen in ages. There was something else about him, Marcus thought. He didn't really 'think' it, he just felt it instantly: he's lonely, like me. I want to know him.

Telemachus was a lot less pleased. He didn't want some child to baby-sit him! He had come to this frontier, to this fort, to his father, to learn to fight. The last thing he wanted, on his first day on the border, was to befriend a boy his brother's age whose tribe was friendly to Rome!

'Hello,' Bran said, suddenly embarrassed and unsure to whom he was meant to be speaking.

'Hello!' Marcus jumped in.

Everyone laughed quietly – exactly the reaction that Telemachus expected and hated. Marcus was hardly aware of it, however, nor was Bran. Immediately they saw they were the same sort, which made the adults smile more.

Gaius could see that Telemachus wanted nothing to do with these two younger boys, so he said, 'Bran, would you show Marcus around the fort and *vicus*? Remember this is his first day here. He has been travelling and may be tired.'

Tired, Marcus thought. The idea was impossible. The two boys grinned at each other. He turned to head out with his new friend.

'Marcus,' his mother spoke sternly but quietly.

'I'm sorry. Father, please may I go out with Bran? It is very good to see you and finally to be at Vercovicium. Thank you for calling us up here.'

'Thank you, Marcus. Yes, you may.' But his look told them not to leave yet.

The boys stood poised like dogs about to bolt out.

'Would you like to join them, Telemachus?' his mother asked, having missed the body language read by Gaius.

'No, thank you, Mother,' Telemachus solemnly replied,

keeping his face as impassive as he could while boiling with rage at the idea that he should spend time with little boys.

'Would you like to tour the fort and area yourself?' Gaius began to suggest, when suddenly a frontier scout arrived at the door of the Praetorium. Immediately the mood changed. 'Claudia, I must return to matters of the fort now, I regret to say, but before I go I would like to introduce Grumio to you. Grumio is a *veteranus* now, but he was an extraordinary scout, able to follow a trail and find the enemy in any land, under even the worst of circumstances.' He fixed his eyes on Claudia. 'He was a brilliant scout. He is from Baetica, in the same land but far south of Tarraconesis Hispania, and his Latin somehow never became standard.'

Claudia nodded agreeably. She wondered why Gaius was making such a fuss about this elderly scout.

Slowly, out from behind the cluster of the family came an old man. He walked with a roll to his hips, was stooped, had a tanned, weathered complexion, dark brows but white hair. He stopped before Gaius and saluted neatly, smartly, then went up to Claudia, cradled her hand in his and kissed it. The company, at first impressed, then was surprised and a little embarrassed.

'Welcome, madam,' he stammered nervously. 'Welcome. Yes. Me too, I no from Britannia. I Baetica. *Veteranus.* Plenty year in legions. Oh, plenty, plenty. No fight now. Gardie. Gardie.' He smiled earnestly, peering into her face for help.

Claudia's eyes had widened just perceptibly. She looked

over at Gaius, who, to her surprise, was standing back a bit, the way he did when he allowed someone else to take the centre. He respects him, she saw, but why? Why would he introduce today, our arrival day, the gardener?

Then Gaius spoke: 'Grumio is invaluable in our Praetorium's courtyard garden. He has created a refuge there from the cold north wind. I won't spoil his surprise for you, but I trust you will be very pleased.'

'Plenty flowers here, madam,' Grumio interrupted. 'And in market, fruiii,' he whistled, 'and vegetables. Oh, yes! Plenty good in Britannia. I like,' he assured her. 'Black-berries, strawberries – plenty berries. Oh, yes. I get them for you! I show boys market?' He raised his eyebrows, revealing terrified eyes beneath bushy, old man's eyebrows.

The boys caught that terror and stiffened.

Claudia felt their reaction and responded. 'Thank you, Grumio. I look forward to seeing our garden and am very interested in the market, as are the boys, I'm sure.' She shot a warning look at both boys. After Brigit, here is another mystery, she thought. 'But now I know the Commander must leave us, and Bran and Marcus must be allowed to go and explore. I'm sure Telemachus can find his own way,' she said, casting him a glance that told him to get along and not to mope. 'I would be grateful now to unpack and settle in the Praetorium.' She smiled graciously at the company. Again, as she had upon greeting Gaius, she gracefully bowed to her husband and nodded to his men. In a flash the waiting room was empty of everyone but the two women.

THE WALL

'Would you care to see the Praetorium first, madam?' Brigit asked.

'Yes, thank you, Brigit.'

The two ladies left the reception rooms and turned on to the staircase that rose up to the first floor, chatting as they climbed. Claudia had dismissed her servants and attendants, simply wanting a quiet tour of the Praetorium now with Brigit.

Claudia spoke first: 'I have heard that the weather in Britannia is horrible, though in our travels up the country these past few weeks we have had beautiful weather.'

'Summer is often beautiful, but it is true there is much rain and darkness, and it is cold the entire year.' Brigit laughed. 'Life up here is difficult, for anyone, I think, but especially for a lady.'

'Why?' asked Claudia, with a hint of trepidation. 'Haven't other fort commanders brought their wives?'

'Yes, or they plan to, as soon as their *praetoria* are finished.' Brigit was solemn. 'The wife of the Prefect at the fort Vindolanda recently died in childbirth, or else you would have had her for a very good and close neighbour. Vindolanda is only one mile south of here.'

Why Claudia had come to the Wall interested Brigit a good deal. After all, she had come to Brigantia from Rome of her own accord too. One of us is following a man and one looking for a man, she thought. Her face darkened: she has a man and she is Roman, I have not got a man and I am not Roman. I am neither Roman nor Brigante. She quickly looked at Claudia, then remembered the boys and Gaius. She was cowed by them, but attracted too. I want to belong, she thought.

Meanwhile, Bran and Marcus were running along the top of the ten-foot-wide Wall, roaring with laughter. The Wall wound up to the west from Vercovicium and down to the east. They had climbed the steps from within the fort, hallooing the sentries on their way. The soldiers smiled at them, pleased to see children in their men-only world. Marcus loved the strong wind in his hair. He had completely forgotten about the tattooed warrior he'd seen on the road and all the mysterious farmers he kept seeing in the distance. He ran and ran, pumping his knees up as high as Bran did. They were both very good athletes.

Telemachus saw them on top of the Wall as he walked away, heading east. It wasn't so long ago that he too would have loved such a run, after days, weeks, in that mule cart. It wasn't what he wanted now, though. He wanted to look around, to be left alone, not to be laughed at.

Looking out of one of the Praetorium's windows, Claudia also saw the boys running along the Wall. She smiled to see Marcus so energetic and happy, and wondered where Telemachus was. He's all right, she thought. He's simply growing up. She suggested Brigit show her the Wall. They set off along the main street of the fort, both looking down, not giving a rude legionary or auxiliary any chance to look directly into their eyes. Each pulled her light scarf across the lower half of her face and held the shawl at her ear. Brigit's red shawl flapped like a flag behind her, as though rallying troops, Claudia thought. She felt threatened by the presence of so many men. The memory of Marcus's alarm this afternoon sprang into her mind. She promised herself she would tell Gaius about Marcus's strange visions. They had happened only in Britannia and mostly in the north. My poor baby is somehow overwrought, though one would never know it to see him now, she thought, smiling.

Brigit turned left, on to the Via Principalis, and led the way up the steep slope towards the northern perimeter of the fort, built directly into the Wall. Claudia had to work hard to keep up as they climbed the slope. Even with the cobblestoned surface, it was difficult to walk quickly. They were approaching the Wall. From a distance, it looked like an ordinary fort wall, though very tall. Yet as she grew closer, she had to throw back her head to see the top of it. 'This must be the height of a three-storey building,' she exclaimed in wonder. Bending her head further back, she saw the crenellations, and a few sentries' faces peering down at her, and then the vast sky, covering everything, filling her vision. That sky is huge, she thought. She was scared and exhilarated. She felt as if she were climbing up the back of something alive and massive and dangerous. After passing a huge granary, they arrived at the guardhouse double doors. 'Come,' Brigit whispered.

The auxiliaries in the guardhouse, four altogether, two at the inside double doors and two at the outside double doors, stepped back to let them pass. The cobblestones were covered with mud and animal dung. But the ladies moved confidently to give the impression that they were busy in their own lives, which had nothing to do with the men's. This was an invisible shield that separated them from the men and keeping that shield up was of the greatest importance. The guards swung open the inner doors, allowing the women into the dark, high-ceilinged but cramped vestibule, and the next set of guards swung open the outer doors.

'Welcome to the land of the Brigantes!' one guard boomed.

'The land of the Selgovae and the Votadini,' the other corrected, in a tone that was deferential and polite to Claudia but conveyed contempt for the native tribes.

'Oh, the land of *Caledonia*,' his partner announced, giving a quick conspiratorial nod to his mate.

Claudia froze. The wind blew her hair straight back, whipped her soft gown against her body and repeatedly snapped the flowing shawl behind her. In front of her was nothing – air – the drop of a sharp, sheer cliff. Carrion crows, screeching, wheeled far below her. She forced herself to look. Dimly, far in the distance, she made out hills, woods, maybe forests. Closer to the fort she saw miles of treeless, bare ground, empty of farms, livestock or people. The land undulated gently and she had the disconcerting sense that it rolled away from her, travelling up the long, slow slope. Up? she thought. Away from me? Then the land goes north! There is much more for the army to conquer, she realized with a jolt. She heard the hungry cawing of the crows as they circled above her head, looking for sheep.

A narrow sheep path led away from the guardhouse and clung to the side of the cliff. She looked left and right, and saw that the Wall was built upon a cliff which itself seemed to travel east to west across Britannia. The cliff of black stone looked almost like a huge ocean wave poised just at the top of its curl. And on top of that rose Hadrian's Wall! As far as she could see, in each direction, the Wall, painted white, dominated the countryside. She felt dizzy, as though she, on top of the Wall, on top of the gigantic wave, were about to be carried on a violent surge of ocean into Caledonia.

Somewhere near her, not at this guardhouse but close by, on the top of the Wall, she heard a jubilant Marcus yelling fearlessly into the wind.

'We've come to the edge of the Empire,' Marcus was bellowing at the top of his lungs. 'The e-d-g-e of the EMPIRE,' he trumpeted. 'Cock-a-doodle-do!' She could hear Bran roaring with laughter, clearly pleased with his new friend. 'COCK-A-DOODLE-DO,' they both yelled in unrestrained delight.

THE BATHS

Telemachus strolled out of the Praetorium. He wanted to get as far away as possible from Marcus and Bran, from Grumio, and from his mother and Brigit.

He found some relief just walking by himself amidst a

crowd of men. He glanced up to the sky quickly, to see the position of the sun in order to gauge the time, and was shocked to see how vast and blue the sky was. I'm really at the top of the earth, he thought. It was now a beautiful summer's day with a warm breeze. He kept his eyes down as he walked, not from shyness or to avoid the sky, but because he was thinking about his father and wondering what impression he had made upon him. Now that he had seen his father again, after so long, he knew that he wanted to be a soldier, a commander. From his mother's side, he could claim to be a member of the senatorial class and as such might aim to command legions or become a provincial governor. His father was of the slightly lower equestrian class. He had done well to become prefect of a fort. Telemachus admired his father and wanted to achieve at least what he had so far achieved; and he knew his father had greater ambitions, perhaps even one day to become prefect of an *ala milliaria*, appointed personally by the Emperor. Telemachus wanted to make his father proud of him.

He crossed through the east gatehouse, with the soldiers hardly noticing him, and walked on past some simple stone farmhouses with pitched, wooden-shingled roofs. When he glanced up, he saw clouds of dark smoke rising and recognized, with delight, Vercovicium's bathhouse. That's what I need, he thought, perking up, a good steam.

In the bathhouse, Telemachus hung his clothes in a niche in the wall and, walking through the cold room, took a seat on a bench in the hot steam room. He waited for a servant to approach him and anoint him with the warm, sweet oil. His mood was definitely lightening. Here he was a man among men. Undressed, he hoped an officer couldn't be distinguished from an auxiliary or a legionary. No one would know he was the son of the Prefect and not a soldier. He glanced at the other men's bodies. Well, they can see I'm younger than most, he thought defensively. Almost all the men there – five in this room, and he could see about five in the next – were much taller, stronger and more developed than he was. Many had blond or light-brown hair, blue eyes and beards! They weren't Romans. Then he remembered: Nervii and Tungrians, peoples whose lands were near the Batavii. Of course. His spirits sank. His father was Batavian, but he did not look like a low-country, northern German. Telemachus realized he stood out, not only as younger but as Roman and smaller. What a terrible day, he thought.

He walked through the arched door into the cold room and crossed to the refreshing cold pool. A group of scouts sat around its edge, chatting. Conscious of their eyes on him, he slipped into the plunge pool and sat in the freezing water. Immediately a slave poured cold water over his head and back. He gasped; it felt like ice. Trying not to shiver, he got as quickly as he could into the *tepidarium*, where the warm steam soon began to thaw his muscles. He knew the scouts were called *areani*, 'the eyes of the army', but wished they wouldn't look at his skinny, shivering back or his face, wet and still without any facial hair. They did, though, and then looked at each other and smiled. They knew the Prefect's family, his wife and two sons, had just arrived.

This must be the older boy, trying to avoid embarrassing questions. They ducked their heads to hide their amusement.

Just then a slave approached Telemachus, bearing an elegant glass bath flask with outlines of grapes and vines pressed into its surface. The flask had been uncorked and Telemachus caught a whiff of roses, lavender and lilies. He knew that oil of lily was used by soldiers to ease wounds and clear the skin (the only wounds I've got are from the rough leather seating in the cart, he thought, clamping his jaw). The rose and lavender oils were soothing, especially for headaches. He lay on a padded table, where the slave rubbed him down with the oils. His muscles began to relax and he forgot about the day of travelling. He then slipped on a pair of wooden-soled sandals and entered the steam room, where four Tungrians were sitting and laughing in the hot plunge pool. He sat quietly along the wall on a stone bench. Steaming was exactly what he needed, he thought, as he began to dream about the waves of hills they'd travelled over that day. His reverie was interrupted by the Tungrians' coarse laughter. As they laughed, they looked around at the new arrival and, to Telemachus's dismay, instantly grew quiet. They know I'm not a soldier and don't belong here, he thought. They're going to question me. To avoid that indignity, he rose and left the room.

He walked to the cool fountain set in the semicircular apse, the domed section of the room, rinsed his face in fresh, cold water and returned to the cold room, leaving his sandals at the arched door. Against the wall of the cold room he saw an altar, 'To the holy goddess Fortuna Conservatrix'. The altar was of stone, almost to his waist in height and in three tiers. Scrolls were carved into the top tier and the inscription into the middle one. He paused and mused on how soldiers liked to dedicate their altars in bathhouses to Fortuna. He shrugged and turned to find the slave who would scrape off the oils and dirt with his strigil. Bracing himself against the pleasant tug and scrape of the strigil, as his arms, back and legs were firmly cleaned, his mood lightened. Afterwards, he finished his cleansing by walking straight into the plunge pool and sitting in the freezing water.

The same *areani* were there, talking. They must have been a long time in the army, Telemachus thought, for they speak Latin together, not German. He knew that everyone in the army – auxiliaries from all over the Empire – had to speak Latin, for that was their uniting language. He kept his face impassive and his eyes focused on the middle distance so they would not suspect he was eavesdropping. Again, he missed their quickly exchanged looks and the tacit agreement to speak before their Prefect's son. He did feel ridiculous, this slender, wet pup in the middle of a pack of strong, battle-worn scouts, but what could he do? The men were solemn and talking quietly.

'I don't like it,' grumbled a young *areanus*.

'No one does,' an older man broke in impatiently. 'Those are orders – from the Emperor.'

'But I don't like going north every day on patrol. I know we have forts up there, lots of them, and roads to connect them. But I still feel exposed. And for what? We aren't taking the north, so why patrol it? I'd rather get sent to Germania. That's where the real fighting is! A soldier can die with dignity there, not like here, with an arrow in the back.'

The other *areani* growled in agreement and shifted on the marble bench.

'We'll do what we're told. That's it,' the older one commanded. 'It's not up to the likes of us to double-think the Emperor. We're here from Tungria.' He looked around the group, all of whom nodded. 'We'll fight wherever we're stationed. We'll do our Batavian prefect proud and retire with Roman citizenship and a pension for life. Now that's not bad, is it? It's worth a couple of years of dull patrols.'

The group agreed, leaving the young one still dissatisfied. Two men glanced over at Telemachus, well aware that he was listening and might report their conversation. They cast warning looks at the young one, who just threw back his head in cross defiance.

Telemachus quietly pondered this.

'Anyway, these patrols might be dull, but they aren't senseless,' a third *areanus* added, 'particularly when we patrol in the west, near Blatobulgium. You know, we gave away some Novantae territory to the Brigantes –'

'Yes, good farming land, used to buy off the Brigantes so they'd be a barrier between us and the Novantae,' the young soldier interrupted, showing off his knowledge.

The others just looked at him.

'The Novantae are not pleased and want us out of here,' the older man continued. 'There's rebellion in the air.'

The group fell silent. Though worried, they trusted in the power of their divine Emperor Hadrian, and in their own gods, whether Roman, like Jupiter, Juno and Minerva, or eastern, like Mithras, Cybele and her young consort, Attis. If the Britons wanted the Romans out of north Britannia, this was a solemn matter that only the Emperor could understand and resolve. They would follow their orders and trust that their magic was more powerful.

'At least we can be sure of one thing. If there's any fighting to be done, it'll be done by us miserable infantry and not by those braggarts on horseback!' Growls of agreement filled the *frigidarium*. 'The cavalry never take risks. It'll be us facing the Novantae!' More deep-voiced agreement.

The men shifted their big muscled bodies as they sat on the bench, talking about what help they could count on getting from the Brigantes. Telemachus could tell they were preparing to end their visit to the baths. He used this moment in the conversation to slip out of the plunge pool and return to the changing room, where he retrieved his clothes and left the bathhouse. There was much to think about. It was a very different world up here.

2 GOOD AND BAD TROUBLE

BRAN'S HOME

Days passed quickly in the lovely north Britannian summer. Bran came nearly every day to Vercovicium, where he and Marcus played, sometimes along the Wall, sometimes in the stables, or watched the auxiliaries practising on the parade ground. Even Telemachus had to admit the sun was warm and the sky magnificent up there, on top of the world. The wind blew the clouds flying across the sky faster than a horse could run. He liked to lie on the spongy grass beside the Wall and watch the wind through the cloud shapes.

Claudia was wary of allowing the boys to leave the fort, but finally, after they had been there almost a month, she relented. Immediately Marcus asked if he could go to Bran's house in his settlement, and got permission. The next day, when Bran arrived, the boys conferred and turned, running down the causeway, away from the Wall and into the valley. Bran led the way across the Military Road and back up the opposite side of the valley, on to his settlement's hill.

He took Marcus along a lively trail to reach his family's settlement. Marcus loved running on this land. It felt smooth and bouncy under his feet because of the moss and thick grass. He thought this effect was magical. At the top of the next hill, Bran stopped. They could see a settlement of round stone huts, encircled by a double enclosure of deep earthwork ditches. There were five thatched houses in the middle, each with a path leading to it. How funny, Marcus thought. First you walk up the hill, then climb over the ditches, then get to the enclosed area at the top and finally choose one path to take you to the hut you want. Don't they worry about cold winds and rain? Why not build in the hollow of the hills, as we do? But there was no time to ask Bran as he had already flung himself down this last dip and was running up the hill towards the settlement.

Marcus pelted after him, filled again with the joy of running and falling and running. As they got to the first enclosure, his heart sank, for the trench was about twenty feet deep, with more earth mounded up on the far side. Bran charged around the enclosure and, to Marcus's dismay, disappeared into a concealed entrance. But the race was on and Marcus tore after him. Just as he caught up with Bran, he saw they were facing another heaped-up circular earthen trench. Bran, not pausing for breath, dashed around the other way and disappeared inside another concealed opening. Marcus followed, feeling a little uneasy. This was, after all, a native settlement. Still, he trusted Bran and so carried on.

Inside was odd. A drystone wall above, as tall as he was, surrounded the huts and a path of paving stones led to each of them. Otherwise the ground was muddy and rocky.

Smoke seeped out from the top of the thatch, even though there didn't seem to be holes there. Cows, pigs, sheep, goats, dogs and horses were penned up in various smaller walled enclosures. Marcus could see a man inside one hut standing by a blazing fire, pounding a small piece of metal with a heavy hammer. Several old women were also visible inside another hut, on their knees, rocking back and forth, grinding corn in small querns. When everyone turned to see who the new boy was – 'and a Roman boy', he felt sure they were thinking – he was overwhelmed with embarrassment. Bran forged confidently ahead to one of the huts. Marcus tried to walk as confidently after him.

Suddenly Bran began shouting and seemed to be calling to someone. As he spoke in his own language, Marcus had no idea what he was saying. He knew he was speaking some kind of Celtic tongue. At least they're happy sounds, whatever he's saying, he thought. A strong-looking red-haired woman came out of Bran's hut. Her relaxed manner and gentle smile calmed Marcus. She had a presence that he knew right away to respect and obey. Coming out of her roundhouse, in her settlement, on her hill, in her land, she welcomed him, and for the first time since he left Rome he felt truly safe.

Speaking in Latin, she greeted him. 'Welcome. I am Modron, Bran's mother. Have you a name?' she asked, confidently but quietly.

'Marcus Decimus Rufinus,' he replied, showing his manners by presenting her with a perfectly impassive, unseeing, frozen face.

Bran's mother looked at this twelve-year-old Roman statue and smiled again. 'Then welcome, Marcus Decimus Rufinus, to the home of Bran of the Brigantes.'

Remembering his manners, Bran now spoke only in Latin: 'Mother, may I take Marcus inside and show him my things?'

And his mother replied in Latin. 'Yes, of course. I'm weaving today at the loom and you won't be in my way.'

Bran led Marcus inside the hut.

'But you will be in mine,' a sharp, teasing voice called out from within the roundhouse.

Alarmed, Marcus looked at Bran, whose face suddenly had darkened. 'Is she home, then?' he asked his mother.

Modron just gave him a wry, amused look and turned back into the house, leading the boys. Unsettled, Marcus followed.

Immediately his senses were accosted by surprises. Inside, the house was dark except for the strong fire in its centre. His eyes began to sting from the smoke and he tripped a little over things he couldn't see. As his eyes grew accustomed to the firelight, he looked around and began to make out his surroundings. The hut was much bigger than it had seemed from the outside. Huge beams supported a conical thatch that towered above his head. He looked up and up, trying to see the top, until he almost fell over. Bran laughed. High, high above their heads, right at the very top of the conical roof, animal carcasses were hanging from the ceiling. 'The smoke from the fire rises, right to that point, and is cooking them!' he murmured aloud. And the smoke at the bottom of the room isn't all that thick, he noted, amazed. A fierce fire blazed in the middle of the hut. Suspended over it was an iron spit, empty now but clearly capable of holding a massive piece of meat or a heavy cauldron. A wicker wall ran around the inside of the hut. Marcus jumped as he saw moving shadows in the passage between the wicker and the hut's outside wall.

'Don't worry. That's just our cows. They're safe there and we all get warm off each other,' Bran explained.

Just then a cow let loose a series of plops. Both boys roared with laughter.

'Like the latrine in a fort,' Marcus joked. 'Your one cow makes a smell as bad as thirty soldiers together.'

'How about thirty cows at one time?' Bran asked.

More laughter.

Then something very fast moved out of the darkness straight at the boys. Marcus was terrified. Thumping down on to a low wooden stool was a girl a little older than the boys. They looked at her in silence, Bran in disgust and Marcus in amazement. A nimbus of flaming red hair surrounded her head like a cloud of fire. Her skin was whiter than any statue of Juno or Venus. In a finely chiselled face, with a delicate jaw and red lips, her huge brown eyes seemed to cast a spell over him. He couldn't move.

'Oh, go away, Rhiannon!' Bran hissed.

Marcus stared at his friend.

'Is this your new Roman friend? Hello. I am Bran's sister. My name is Rhiannon, as you may have guessed. And I'm sure you're very impressed with our Latin. Not every

Brigante can rattle away in our conquerors' tongue as we can, eh, Bran?'

Although there was a smile on her face as she said this, Marcus felt a dart in her words. He didn't know how to respond.

'Shut up, Rhiannon!' Bran growled more loudly.

'Too bad you can't talk, Roman boy,' she said, holding his alarmed attention. 'Shall I tell you why our Latin is so good? Brigit, your mother's companion, is our relative and she has taught us.'

The safe feeling that Modron had given Marcus was gone, but he didn't know what to do about it.

'Yes! I mean no, I didn't know Brigit was your relative . . .'

'What a confusion! Yes-no! I always thought Romans were so logical and liked to set forth everything in a straight line or at right angles. You're blessed with a Brigantian swirl to your answers, boy.' Her tone sounded less harsh than her words and her face looked more amused than hostile.

Modron was about to speak when Bran burst out, 'Rhiannon, leave Marcus and me alone! We weren't bothering you. And you, the perfect Brigante, aren't being very hospitable,' he snarled. 'You're rude to everybody – to anyone who comes to our home. You're rude to our men, to the soldiers, to anyone I bring home.' His tone hovered between being insulting and whining.

'This is true.' She paused, embarrassed. 'You're right and I apologize. Marcus, as I guess that's your name, welcome. And I'm sorry I was so rude. I get used to struggling with this hideous Bran here and forget that maybe all boys his age aren't monsters.' By now, the smile in her eyes had lit up her lovely face and Marcus felt uncomfortable just looking at her. She turned to face Bran and again spoke darkly: 'As for being rude to everyone, Bran, that's none of your business. If I don't want people to come to this house, that's up to me.'

'It isn't "people" you don't want,' Bran muttered beneath his breath.

Rhiannon glowered at him. Marcus didn't know what Bran meant, but he recognized all the signs of a fight and rushed in to save his new friend.

'Oh,' he faltered, trying to think of some reply, 'I don't have a sister . . .'

'What do you have?' she snapped.

'A big brother. Fifteen. Just as irritating, I suppose, as a little brother!' He knew she had been teasing him and he wanted to please her. He also wanted to distract her from the argument with Bran.

'Is he here too?' she asked, alarmed, looking around the room.

Yet another change in her tone, Marcus thought with surprise. She certainly changes quickly. Now she's worried and curious. 'Yes,' he said, 'but not right in this room.'

Before Rhiannon could speak again, Modron intervened with a sharp call: 'Rhiannon.'

She jumped up and Marcus stared at her for the briefest moment. His eyes caught sight of a broad bangle of finely polished bronze at her wrist. She spun on her heel then, so

40

he couldn't see her front any more, but now he could see her amazing red hair. There are beads woven into her hair, he exclaimed to himself. Scattered all over!

Marcus was about to say, 'She's a bit rough on people, isn't she?' when Bran got up too and crossed the room to sit on a stone bench against the wicker. His chin was down on his chest and his shoulders hunched. Marcus understood he did not want to talk about his sister. Instead, Bran dug behind the bench and pulled out a leather tie-string bag, motioning for Marcus to come and sit beside him. Marcus chose his steps carefully on the hard-pressed earth floor. He soon reached Bran's bench and sat beside him.

'Look,' Bran said, as out of the bag tumbled six metal shapes, each the size of his palm. He offered one to Marcus, who took it and turned towards the fire to get a better view.

Marcus held up a cast bronze ring. The fire's glow lit up a red glass inlay, set around elegant swirls of bronze.

'It's part of a horse harness,' Bran answered evenly. 'Here is the rest.'

With terrific pride he passed one harness ring after another to Marcus, who was amazed, rapt with attention. Each one was more stunning than the last. All were cast bronze and inlaid with glass, some flared red, some blue, yellow and white. A wonderful horse's bit was decorated with opaque red glass balls, themselves inlaid with four blue flower petals in glass. Another piece was decorated with the most intricate interweaving of lines and shapes that Marcus had ever seen. To follow one line he had to turn his head up and sideways and down, and even then he lost its swoop as his eye careened off along another curving line. These pieces were unlike anything he had seen in all his days of admiring Roman armour.

'Here's a cake of raw opaque glass. See? That's where they get the red.'

Bran put into Marcus's cupped hands a heavy ash-covered chunk of glass. Marcus turned it towards the light and stared. Here was pure, solid fire.

'Who made these?' he asked, perplexed but vaguely expecting some answer like Mesopotamians or artisans from Aegyptus.

'Brigantes. Did you see that man working by the fire at the settlement's entrance? He can make these. But other tribes here can make them too. The ones around here, like the Votadini, the Selgovae, the Parisi, they can. But I've seen pieces done by tribes down south that are just as good. All our tribes are known for their metalwork.' He looked directly at Marcus, making Marcus want to shrink back slightly. 'That's what we care about, more than buildings or roads or walls or whatever.'

His words seemed to jab at Marcus simply for being a Roman. He spluttered an answer, saying, 'Well, buildings and towns and bridges and things are good to have. Do you think we have to choose?' He looked earnestly at Bran.

'I don't know,' Bran said, shrugging and looking quickly back at Marcus. 'I don't suppose we have to choose, but why then did my people get so good at metalwork and yours at . . . building things? How did that happen?'

Marcus didn't have any answers so he dropped his head.

Seeing his reaction, Bran pulled the mood back up, saying, 'Look at these. They're my favourites.' This time he dug back to the left of the stone bench and pulled out a different leather bag. He smiled as he passed one piece to Marcus.

Marcus burst out laughing. 'It's a horse! Look how sad he is! He looks like he's had too much wine!' Both boys relaxed, chuckling. 'Is he another harness part?'

'Yes. He's made of sheet bronze,' Bran boasted.

'What is this, then?' Marcus looked more closely at two more masks, each one about as long as his longest finger. 'Oh, I see! They're men's faces! Look! They've got moustaches and holes for eyes! They're Brigantes! These are wonderful, Bran.'

Bran was very pleased with this new friend's reaction to the harness pieces. He carefully put away the jewelled bronzes in their bag, and the mask plaques in their bag, and stored the bags back in their respective hiding places.

Now that things felt calm again, Marcus decided to risk asking about Rhiannon. 'Is Rhiannon always . . . that way?' he asked Bran.

'Well, not to people generally. She just doesn't like Romans at all or boys much. You qualify in two areas!' He smiled. 'You see, my father was killed in a skirmish. He was fighting alongside the Romans against a combined tribal attack of the Selgovae and the Novantae. It was just after Hadrian became Emperor. I was two. I don't remember him really at all, but my sister was five at the time and she can remember him. He was on the Romans' side, but she still blames the Romans for the whole situation. If they hadn't come, there wouldn't have been that tribal warfare.'

Marcus didn't know where to look, so kept his face turned down. He was thinking about what Bran had just said.

'Are the Novantae and the Selgovae friendly with the Brigantes? I mean ... if the Romans hadn't come along?' Marcus asked.

Bran scrunched his face up and scowled. 'No, not really. Our clans are related and we're all people of this area. But the tribes steal cattle and take over land from each other all the time. I wouldn't call them friendly.'

'So Rhiannon likes Brigantes?' Marcus shyly continued.

'No.'

'Why not?' He knew he was asking rather personal questions and his brow furrowed with the uncertainty of it all. But he was trying as much to understand the tribal politics as this odd girl, so he pushed on.

Bran sighed. 'She blames the Brigante men for not helping the Romans more when they came to conquer. Lots of different tribes, or parts of tribes, resisted the Romans – some Brigantes, the Novantae, the Selgovae, and members of other tribes, like the Votadini. If more had helped, maybe our father wouldn't have been killed.' He looked sideways at Marcus.

'That doesn't make any sense. He could have died in any battle, whatever the odds.' Marcus looked questioningly at Bran.

'I know.'

The two exchanged looks.

'I do have a father, of course ... well, sort of,' Marcus went on, but suddenly he wasn't sure if he was setting out to make a joke or revealing something very personal about himself.

'What do you mean?' Bran asked.

'Oh, nothing. I have a father, certainly.' He stopped, and both boys settled their backs more deeply against the roundhouse wall. 'But all my life I've hardly seen him. He's been away on the Dacian campaign. I'm still not sure what it's going to be like up here, if I'll see much of him ... if it'll work out.' He ground to a halt.

'If what'll work out?' Bran pushed.

'If ... oh, a lot of "if"s. I don't know.' Marcus was suddenly impatient. Why was he telling all this to a relative stranger? He pulled himself off the bench and began to kick at the earth floor.

Bran watched him closely. 'Let's go to that metal-worker's roundhouse, just over there.' He pointed.

Marcus nodded and they started off. As they walked, Bran started talking about himself. It seemed only fair as Marcus had just told him some things. 'The legionaries and auxiliaries always treated me ... well, babied me really, probably because they missed their own sons. And I wonder if my father might have been like them. I spend most of my time around the legionaries, as they build forts and roads and things, or around the auxiliaries in the exercise yard, if they let me. I always used to think that the Wall and all the forts were built to avenge my father's death.' He turned and smiled awkwardly.

Marcus just nodded and kept looking down. He couldn't think of anything to say. Then he remembered the beads in Rhiannon's hair and asked, 'Why does your sister wear her hair huge, like a massive red cloud, and with beads in it? Everyone will look at her.'

Bran burst out laughing. This explosion surprised Marcus and was contagious. A huge smile spread across his face, rearranging all his features once again into those of a confident, robust, mischievous boy of twelve.

'She's an idiot, isn't she?' Bran answered. 'You got her right on your first visit!'

And both boys threw back their heads and laughed. They had Rhiannon figured out.

'I liked your mother, Bran,' Marcus added.

'Oh, she's all right,' Bran agreed. 'When my father died she inherited the land, our cows, two horses, the house and the loom. She's taken care of us completely on her own. She weaves the best woollen fabrics in the area and sells them down at the market in Coria. She's very respected in our tribe, you know,' he said, checking Marcus's face to see that this information had registered appropriately. But Marcus had got stuck on one part of Bran's speech.

'She inherited? She? A woman inherited?' Marcus couldn't believe his ears. No Roman woman would ever inherit – it was inconceivable.

Bran looked confused.

'Women aren't allowed by Roman law to inherit,'

Marcus announced. 'The men of the family have to look after them. Did she have a father or any brothers?' He looked earnestly and with growing disapproval into this Brigante's face. Uncivilized, he remembered.

Bran had become agitated. 'What? Are you mad? Women run everything around here. They are in charge of the home, they often till the fields, they hunt, they trade at the markets, they fight in battles . . .'

'They what?' Now Marcus was genuinely shocked. 'They fight in battles?' His eyes were wide. His mind filled with visions of the legionaries practising for months, years, to be able to act as one articulated body in battle, under strictest discipline, relentlessly closing in on and destroying the enemy. Imagining a woman or women among them was too strange. He had to show Bran how ridiculous this idea was. 'Think of Rhiannon in battle,' he nearly shouted, the absurdity of it forcing gulps of furious laughter to bubble up his throat.

Bran stopped dead still and looked at this Roman boy. He no longer felt like laughing. Waves of loyalty to his sister and his tribe's ways rolled through his body. 'She would swing the axe and inflict as many gashes and spill as much blood as the best warrior.'

Through Bran's eyes Marcus saw Rhiannon in battle and grew completely confused. Could women do battle? he wondered. Could they? What an idea. He had much to learn about these Brigantes. The boys walked on to the metalworker's roundhouse.

MOTHER AND DAUGHTER

After the boys left the roundhouse, Rhiannon returned and sat near her mother. 'Rhiannon,' her mother said in a low voice. She sighed and, laying the little wooden shuttle on the stretched wool threads, dropped her hands in her lap. 'How is it that everyone can see the benefit of the Roman occupation but my daughter?'

'Could it be because she misses her father?' Rhiannon replied in a tight voice.

On Modron's face intense irritation warred with sorrow. They had had this conversation a hundred times. Rhiannon never relented, always blaming. Of course Modron missed her husband. Raising the children alone hadn't been easy. But her husband had fought for the Empire because their life had been much better under the Romans than it had been before. He and she had seen this, so why couldn't their daughter see it too? Modron tried another approach. 'You would not be Queen Cartimandua, then, eh? No supporting the Romans for you. Does only the anti-Roman blood of her husband run in your veins?' she quietly asked.

'Sixty years ago he resisted the legionaries. I would have fought alongside him!'

'And died with him.'

'Yes,' she proudly proclaimed. 'To keep out the legions, not to have our land cut in two by the Wall, to live with our neighbouring tribes as we have lived with them for thousands of years, yes!'

Modron picked up the shuttle again and began drawing it through the wool threads on her loom. The little iron weights holding each colour clanged against one another. 'You speak foolishness, girl. The days before the Romans were not so peaceful.' She sighed. 'There were no roads as we have now, no trade, no money, no lovely goods from far away, only bartering for essentials. Life was much harder. This was our way of life and our people survived. But it's foolishness not to welcome an improvement when you see it.'

She looked up from her seated position. She saw, beneath that cloud of ginger hair, her lovely daughter's angry, troubled face. Rhiannon was old enough to understand the hypocrisy and greed as well as the honour of the past. She tried again.

'Cartimandua's husband, Venutius, just wanted to hold on to his power, his little kingdom. He didn't care about the Brigantes and their welfare. You misrepresent and glorify the past and deny the present.' Crossness welled up in her and she couldn't resist adding, 'Take greater care with your future!'

'You always talk about money and trade and how well off the clans are now. You think you know what's best for our tribe. Well, maybe the Novantae and Selgovae know better!' Rhiannon tossed her head at her mother, spun on her heel and strode out of the hut.

THE MEETING

Rhiannon had not wanted to hear her mother's words. Her people had lived on this land forever. This was their land. They had farmed here for generations. I miss my father, she thought. 'I miss you, Father,' she whispered.

Running fast, she imagined she was Epona, the horse goddess, the mare-headed mother. When she was a little girl, her father had told her all about Epona and the other goddesses. He had named her Rhiannon after another goddess closely linked with horses. This was Rhiannon's strongest memory of her father and she treasured it. He held her in his arms, as they sat before the roundhouse fire, and told her about Epona's dog that heals and leads people to the Underworld, about her raven, huge and black, which often accompanied her. Epona brought fertility and abundance to the tribe, and she reminded people to honour the beauty, speed, intelligence and bravery of their horses. Some even said Epona's father was a man and her mother a mare. Epona protected the tribe and its territory.

Rhiannon also remembered what her father told her about Coventina, the water spirit, the nymph, healer of the sick, protector against evil, guide to the Underworld and goddess of well-being. Rhiannon looked for her in every spring and pool and stream around her settlement. She made offerings to her, on her name-day and on festivals: little finger-rings, glass beads, one of her own baby teeth, a carved dog of bone.

Just this year, the legionary engineers had enclosed a spring, calling it Coventina's Well. They had lined it with timber, drawing the water away in lead pipes, and built a square stone enclosure, roofless, around it. This spring rose to the surface right near the crest of the black cliff on which the Wall was built. Many men were there, vallum diggers and auxiliaries, so she kept away. One day, I'd like to visit the well and see if I can feel the presence of Coventina, she thought, as she strode along the crest of the hill.

As she hurried away, she sang to herself: I am Rhiannon the heroine, Rhiannon the Brigante. I alone will save our lands from the invaders. She found herself soothed, praying, forgetting to be angry, now running, joyful in her own land. Our gods already heal me, she thought.

She pelted up the slope and down the other side, almost running straight into a boy. By his clothes, his age, his Roman look, this had to be Marcus's older brother, she realized. Still ashamed of her rudeness to Marcus, she disciplined herself to obey the Brigantian rules of hospitality. 'I'm sorry. I hope I didn't startle you?' she asked in her best Latin.

Telemachus did not feel like being polite. What oaf is this? was his first thought. Then his eyes focused. A goddess! I have run into a barbarian goddess! He started to speak: 'I apologize.' He went down on one knee and bowed before her.

This is better, she thought. This is how Romans ought to behave. Thank you, Epona and Coventina! She spoke: 'Rise, Roman. The fault was mine. I know these hills and ought to have been more careful.'

With alarm and embarrassment, Telemachus glanced again at the 'goddess', a mere Brigante girl, he now realized. He pulled himself up to his full height to present himself. 'Telemachus Aurelius Rufinus forgives you and allows you to continue.'

'*I* may continue? *I* am forgiven?'

'Go. Take more care in the future,' he advised.

'Go?' Her voice rose in volume and pitch.

Here was the enemy, rude and obnoxious – her size, her age, not an army but an arrogant boy. Every bit of anger she felt towards Rome boiled up within her and, without quite knowing what she was doing, she flew at him, yanking at his hair and scratching his face. Caught completely off guard, Telemachus went down like a toddler. Instinctively, he fought back, grabbing at her legs as he fell, pulling her to the ground. He felt soft skin and a delicate jawbone, but she fought hard. This didn't feel right at all. As strong as she was, he had no difficulty grabbing both arms and holding her down. He stared at the furious face, a foot away from his, glaring at him. Her cheek was red and had already begun to swell. But that wasn't what he saw. Her colour had been heightened by the fight. Her red hair covered the ground, like a rich carpet beneath her head. White skin, huge brown eyes, elegant lips, red cheeks (here he felt the first pang of remorse) and a heaving bosom, barely visible at the top of her open tunic, combined to increase his discomfort. He let go and leapt up and away, holding himself in readiness for another attack.

She rolled over, jumped up and went at him again. This

time he grabbed her arms as they made for him and wrapped them around her torso. This was marvellously effective at controlling his enemy, but did put him tightly against her body. Suddenly it seemed to him that there was no way to undo the hold without risking another attack. They would have to stay entwined forever. He flushed, and she did too. Now nothing would hold her. With a gigantic burst of strength, she wrenched herself away and ran back three steps, turning with hatred to face him.

'Get out of my land! All things Roman, go! Never come back!'

Departure did seem the preferred course. He settled his wits, double-checked his balance, straightened his tunic, turned and walked away down the slope. Head held high, straight back, a slow step, he trusted his parting impression.

Just then he heard, 'Telemachus! Hello! Telemachus! Wait!' And the happiest, most carefree younger brother in the world jogged and tumbled happily towards him from the crest of the next hill. Bran was standing back, waving goodbye to Marcus. His face too was beaming happiness.

'Damn,' Telemachus cursed, and kept on walking.

THE GARDEN

On the day that Marcus was given permission to visit Bran's settlement, Claudia, Brigit and Grumio were walking slowly, heads down, in the Praetorium's courtyard garden. Claudia's two maidservants walked a few steps behind them. Claudia had a good knowledge of plants, but here many were new to her. Grumio was enjoying teaching her and was especially proud to show off 'his' garden. She enjoyed the order and control a garden gives to a home. In this Praetorium, the two sets of stairs and an upstairs corridor circled the courtyard, allowing light and views to come into the house from between the pillars. She did wonder fleetingly about the famous wind and rain of Britannia, for surely that would come into the house too. But it wasn't a large garden, hidden in the middle of the house, in the middle of the fort, so perhaps not that much wind and rain would come in. At least it gave her and her family some privacy and respite from the military regimentation.

Grumio had done a magnificent job in only two years. There was an extraordinary variety of flowers and plants. As a special surprise for her, he had just finished laying a brick path in a herringbone pattern right up the centre of the courtyard, lining each side with a spiky little green bush called box. He was something of a puzzle, she had been thinking. A brilliant scout once, a talented gardener and a dear, sweet man, but clearly simple. His Latin, no doubt picked up during his childhood in Malaga, was impossible. She knew already that Gaius trusted this funny man. She would watch him carefully, to get to know him better.

'Madam, plenty flowers here. Plenty. Plenty. Many pretty Britannia flowers. Oh, yes. Rome flowers too. Oh, yes. You know, Rome?' he asked, peering anxiously into her eyes.

'Yes, I do recognize some of these, Grumio,' Claudia answered, unable to prevent a whisper of condescension slipping into her tone. 'Oh, they are pretty! So fine and colourful. What are these ones called?' she asked him.

'New you? Bird's-foot trefoil. See, three leaves? Oh, yes,' he answered, delighted to be teaching her something. He made an effort to find more local plants. 'Milkwort,' he continued, pointing. 'No weed, no. Oh, no. Dog violet? You know? All feenished.' He raised his face and upper lip to hiss out this sound. 'All gone. No. But next year, plenty!' He waved his arms in a huge circle. 'And rockrose too. Oh, plenty, like Roma. Oh, yes,' he concluded triumphantly, beaming at her. His face cracked into a huge smile, but his eyes, if one looked keenly and quickly, expressed a flickering alarm and confusion.

Claudia turned away so as not to embarrass or scare him. 'How wonderful to have many violets. I shall like that, Grumio. I would like to fill the Praetorium with them, in wreaths, garlands, along the dining table,' she said, lingering and daydreaming of a first springtime here with armfuls of violets. 'Maybe I can like living here,' she mused. 'Maybe it will be all right.'

Grumio walked alone, behind the two ladies. Anyone able to study his face would have seen calculation. He knew he was old, well beyond usefulness. He wanted to be useful. He seemed established as the gardener. He might also be allowed to teach the Prefect's older boy the ways of scouts. That would be good. The army had been his life. As ever, the prospect of retirement, of living alone, swirled darkly inside him. Why should he return to Baetica? He hadn't lived there for decades. Should he live there, alone? What would be the point? No, he needed to stay connected with the fort, with the army. That was his life. The intelligence that had generated these thoughts darted quickly back behind his tired and worried eyes. He must play the gardener now. He must make sure madam and her friend were pleased.

Brigit walked quietly just behind Claudia. She had left Rome a year ago and felt that these past twelve months had been a whirlwind of getting to know her Brigante cousins. They were not 'barbarians', as her Roman friends said, but neither was their life better than that of the Romans. They lived in wretched hovels, but their life of the imagination – myths, tales, metalwork – was rich, richer than the Romans', she thought. Anyway, she'd felt torn all year, yearning for Rome while deeply wanting to belong here.

In fact, she was scared. She had Roman citizenship but didn't feel Roman. Her blood was Brigantian and she had inherited lands around Eboracum, but she didn't feel a Brigante. She was named after the goddess of the Brigantes, and as a little girl she had dreamed she *was* Brigantia. Yet she was, she thought grimly, like a Roman-styled statuette of Brigantia, not the invisible, true spirit of the goddess, just a clay version of the real thing. Maybe neither culture wanted her – her coldest fear. Maybe she belonged nowhere, would never marry. She pulled her shawl closer around her slender body, nearly folding her ribcage upon itself.

'What are you thinking, Brigit? You are lost to us. I've been speaking to you for a good ten paces,' Claudia said, laughing, feeling relaxed, happy and tired.

Brigit coloured. 'Oh, lots of things, but one is the

pleasure of an ancient treat,' she covered. 'I've collected roses and made an attar for perfumes. When we return to the fort, we can bathe our feet in warm, scented rose water.' She looked calmly at Claudia, with that curiously composed, poised expression Claudia had first noticed upon their introduction.

'That would be wonderful.' Claudia sighed, wondering again what it was about Brigit that made her keep her guard up. Brigit had been nothing but kind to her, yet still Claudia felt reserved. Rearranging her own mood, she joked, 'Even without Marcus and Bran, this has been a long day. Yes, let's go in.'

'You take to fort? Plenty, plenty. Good. Plenty here. Good. Good. Here,' Grumio broke in, as he stooped over and retrieved from behind the box a large trug filled with cuttings of all the flowers and plants they had been discussing. 'Here. Take. Good. Make Praetorium very nice.' He beamed, knowing the pleasure of fresh-cut flowers.

'Oh! Thank you, Grumio. These are beautiful. Thank you,' Claudia replied, while both she and Brigit smiled at the combination of his earnest enthusiasm and curious syntax.

The ladies were amused by his simplicity, and he was amused by theirs. Yes, all three thought, this arrangement of Grumio as the gardener would work out.

Grumio turned again to his garden, leaving them, and muttering to himself, 'Snails ... Oh, no. Slugs. No, no, no. Oh, no.'

The two women, silently accompanied by Claudia's maidservants, slowly ambled back down the brick path, up the two stone steps into the Praetorium's corridor and down towards Claudia's bedroom.

Claudia turned and asked Brigit, 'Shall we soak our feet? But after that, you must go home and I shall then have a long steam, bath and massage before dining with my husband and boys.' Her words showed companionable honesty and made Brigit smile. This was an unusual display of candour for a Roman. 'You know, I've never asked you, where is your home, Brigit?' Claudia asked.

'I live with my cousins in a little farm settlement on the north side of the Wall. We have a strong, good-sized house, a shrine, a corn-drier and a well. We're very modern here, you know!' She smiled, but then wondered why she had just boasted about her cousins' very provincial farm.

The maidservants followed the women along the black-and-ochre-painted hallway and into the bedroom. 'Oh, I do like this room,' Claudia exclaimed. Brigit smiled. Each wall was painted with five panels in four colours. In the room there were a chaise-longue bed, a curved sofa and several chairs dotted about. The floor was a dark blue and felt warm beneath their feet. At least during the winter I shan't be freezing cold in my own bedroom, Claudia thought.

Claudia swirled off her shawl and threw herself down on the chaise. 'Brigit, I'm sorry, but suddenly I am too tired to speak, much less to bathe my feet. I shall just have a massage and then a little nap before dinner.'

'Not at all. Sleep well and . . .'

Claudia was already giving orders to her maidservant and Brigit knew she had been dismissed. Pulling her Roman shawl more tightly around her, she turned to leave, to return to her cousins' farm with its stone floors and fireplace. As she envisioned her bedroom there, in stark contrast to Claudia's, she remembered the bronze hand-mirror she had inherited from her mother, and she from her mother, and she from hers. She loved the basket-weave effect of its decoration, giving the surface the look of a hidden face. 'My culture,' she whispered to herself.

Brigit's cousins' farm was just north of the Wall. It was always a little difficult getting home in the dark, but she knew the way well. She said her goodbyes and left Vercovicium by the north gate, taking the path down the rock cliff to get on to the rolling plain. As she climbed the slope north, her eyes glanced up, into the dark of the northern sky. She shuddered. That was where she never wanted to go: north, into the lands of the Caledonians, beyond the reach of the Empire. She shuddered again but soon came to a small patch of woods. There, surrounded by rich meadows, protected from the northern winds and out of sight of the Wall, was her cousins' solid and prosperous farm.

AT THE PRINCIPIA

Gaius had had a good but busy day. A visit up north to a camp, no horrendous news, no skirmishes, no breakdown of supplies. North, south, east and west were enemies of the Empire, but the fort was still safe. I have enough men, he thought. Enough to hold the fort, probe the north and control the south, as long as nothing goes wrong. The *areani* had warned him of rebel tribes in the north-west, above the Wall, especially the Novantae and the Selgovae.

He was sitting in the Principia. To his left, at the chapel that held the cohort standard and a bust of Hadrian, he heard shouted commands and the stamping of the soldiers' hobnailed sandals as the watch changed. Dinnertime, he thought absently. 'Dinnertime!' he spoke aloud as he remembered his family. A month here and already I am neglecting them! But as he listened to the sounds of the fort, reminding him of the military's exact routines, he was lulled back into his worries. I have a short time to discuss matters with Quintus Valerius before we eat, he reassured himself. He wanted to be with his family, but the affairs of Vercovicium weighed heavily upon him. That's why they shouldn't have come, he scowled. She knows that. Ah, but there we are. We've hardly had a marriage these ten years. Dacia was ruining our family. I want her and I want to oversee the education of my sons, he reminded himself. Well, if I can't come to Rome, Rome must come to me.

Rome really had come to Britannia. The last thirty years had seen two complete defensive systems set in place. First, intersecting the original north–south road, the legionaries built an east–west road across the neck of Britannia, parallel to the vast sweep of a whinstone cliff. Along the road timber forts had been built and signal towers that could be seen one from the other across the breadth of the country. Increasingly over the years, the road had been used to carry thousands of men daily to and fro – their grain, armaments, horses, carts, equipment – right through the valley trough that lay to the south of the huge thrusting rock. And now, up from the valley, parallel to this road, along the cliff, lay the Wall. In under a decade, he reflected proudly, all carved out of the ground, shaped and made. The Wall stands for it all, for the glory of Rome!

Then he sighed and sat for a moment, his mind blank. He was trying not to remember how, over these last fifty years, the Roman legions had marched into the north, well beyond the Wall, established forts, built roads and then marched back down. We did retreat. He sighed again and shifted uneasily in his chair. Well, the Empire needed to pull out the troops to reinforce the Danube.

Gaius shook his head. He had such ambitions for himself and for Rome. That was where his heart was. His gloomy thoughts were interrupted by a welcome sound.

'Prefect!' called a confident, deep voice.

Gaius's face relaxed into a smile as his favourite centurion and greatest help walked in. 'Quintus Valerius! Welcome. I've been expecting you – and brooding again!' To Quintus, more than to anyone, Gaius spoke his mind.

The centurion smiled as he sat down opposite Gaius. Quintus had the kind of body one wouldn't like to challenge. He was of medium height, with broad shoulders, heavy-set and thick-necked. The weathered skin on his face creased into laughter lines as he smiled at his commander and friend. He had big, strong hands that looked capable of securing any action.

He's bothered about the Wall again, Quintus thought.

Wonders if Rome is rewarding him or holding him down. This doubt is hard on a professional soldier – especially one with an aristocratic wife to measure up to! *Eheu!* She is beautiful. Out loud, Quintus said, 'Some more rumbling among the troops about the patrols.'

'We can't allow that, Quintus.' Gaius shot him a look. 'We can't afford to let down our guard.'

'No,' he agreed. 'I have spies among the Brigantes and the Selgovae and the Novantae. I know where the most likely trouble spots will be. You know, I do hear stories of people who swear they've seen spirits. I don't know – *genii loci*, I suppose. I keep a record of every so-called sighting. I can find no pattern. No disrespect to the spirits, sir, but a person who says he has seen spirits gets a big audience and a lot of attention.'

Gaius remembered what Claudia had told him: that Marcus had seen spirits, visions, whatever. He must think about that. Right now, he answered, 'I know. It may well just be story-telling. Still, story-telling can inspire a revolt too.'

'We'll work it all out, sir. Meanwhile, dinner. I need to get to my provisions before some dog from hell steals my food!' The heavy wooden table creaked as he rose.

Gaius followed, and their sandals scraped on the stone floor. Both men stopped before a map pinned with short nails to the wall.

'Grain and pay for five thousand men – cavalry, infantry – is due soon, for us and all the forts west of us along the Wall. And these forts need to hold the Selgovae and the

62

Novantae. Rome isn't wrong about our having enemies to the north, you know. We have to look after our share,' Quintus said, already turning and clearly ready to leave the Principia to get his dinner.

'No, of course we have enemies to the north. The yet-to-be-conquered world is to the north. There –' he waved his arm impatiently above his head – 'is where we are destined to go, always extending the edge of Empire.' He looked fiercely at Quintus, as though daring him to contradict.

'Speaking of unconquered territory,' Quintus replied, looking up at the ceiling and sucking his teeth, 'don't you have a wife next door? The Prefect of Vercovicium with his woman here and he's poring over a map!'

Gaius smiled at his friend. 'True, I'm a lucky man. She isn't always easy, though, my friend. This is a sharp-tongued woman.'

Gaius had half chuckled, but Quintus thought he heard a hint of concern behind his friend's good-humour. 'Ah, well, remember your Hippocrates: "If they become pregnant, they will be cured." Anyway, life for us soldiers will be easier the more you try!'

Laughing, they strolled out together, headed for dinner.

3 DANGEROUS PLAY

SURPRISES AT VERCOVICIUM

For the next three weeks, Claudia wouldn't permit Marcus to visit Bran, or Telemachus to wander about, but insisted they settle into their lessons with their tutor, the Greek slave, Titus Helius. Midsummer had well passed and, back in Rome, their classmates would soon be resuming their schooling, also by private tutors at home. Marcus's task consisted mainly of memorizing extended passages from *The Iliad* and *The Odyssey*. He had to declaim the verses to his tutor, speaking in a dramatic and formal manner. And he had to understand every line of the ancient Greek, being able to explain how it fitted into the tale but also how its meaning applied to daily life.

The wonderfully gory passages appealed to him, as when Achilles' metal spear ripped into a Trojan's flesh:

Achilles lunged [at Demoleon] ...
he stabbed his temple and cleft his helmet's cheekpiece.
None of the bronze plate could hold it – boring
    through
the metal and skull the bronze spearpoint pounded,
Demoleon's brains splattered all inside his casque ...

The splattering of brains *inside* the helmet was very satisfying.

But mostly, rather than think about Achilles, he wanted to run, eat and laugh with his new friend, Bran. Finally his mother gave permission for Bran to spend the day at Vercovicium, sending the invitation through Brigit. Bran arrived, on this late summer morning, delighted to see his Roman friend.

Today would be special. Today the boys planned to explore the whole place on their own. The weather was perfect: huge clouds sped across the vast blue sky, strong breezes blew and every living thing felt comfortable.

As Bran came strolling up the main road through the cluster of houses and shops, Marcus grinned. Steam from the *vicus* bathhouse and smoke from the inn clouded the air, so that Bran seemed to be emerging from an enchanted mist. He and Marcus were well matched in physique – both unusually strong for boys of twelve. Marcus saw that Bran moved like an athlete or a well-conditioned soldier, with a sort of loping gait and perfect balance, his huge feet slightly pigeon-toed.

After three weeks barely allowed out, Marcus could not face going back into the Praetorium. He kept up his pace and ran left, along the wall of his home, and then right, to the entrance of the hospital. Bran followed him into a quiet, small reception room and could see, through the room, a small open courtyard just beyond. With eight hundred men stationed at Vercovicium, a number might be ill on any given day. The central courtyard allowed light and fresh air into every room. They were about to climb an abandoned ladder to explore the storage loft of the building when they heard an auxiliary approaching, so they slipped instead into the empty surgery. There they silently studied the surgical tools that were laid out. Marcus, not content with the wonders displayed, began searching behind the doctor's desk and pulled out a package wrapped securely in leather and tied with leather strings. There was dust on the leather and the strings were stiff with disuse.

'Look at all these odd little spoons and knives. It's as if they are for spreading butter or honey!'

'They're all bronze and specially made,' Bran mused. 'Whoever made them knew exactly what shapes he wanted. But why these shapes?'

The boys gazed at over fifteen different probes, needles, chisels, scalpels and curiously hooked scissors.

'Oh, Bran,' Marcus moaned, just now beginning to use his imagination. 'They're all for poking or pushing or cutting out bits of the body! Scooping, tugging . . .' He began to feel ill. The lines from *The Iliad* floated up in his memory. 'These are for stabbing and cleaving,' he told Bran, turning to look solemnly at him.

'You don't know. You're just trying to scare me,' Bran retorted. He tried not to show Marcus, but these instruments worried him, not just because they were themselves frightening, but because he knew, from his tribe's careful metalwork, that they were used by experienced men. Whoever made them and whoever used them knew a lot more about the human body and how to heal it than even his tribe's wisest wise man. 'Let's go somewhere else,' he said.

They slipped out of the infirmary and, turning left outside the door, began climbing the slope towards the granary. To their surprise, Telemachus and Grumio were walking up the slope too. Marcus saw that Telemachus was utterly miserable and was trying to distance himself from Grumio by lagging a step behind. Grumio, however, looked uncharacteristically purposeful and confident.

'Hello, Telemachus,' called Marcus, with a studied expression that the brothers knew meant, 'What is this exactly?' Bran trailed behind Marcus, interested.

Telemachus and Grumio stopped. 'Grumio is taking me out to the hills above the fort, north of the Wall, to show me how to scout,' he answered levelly. He knew Marcus would realize that this was their father's idea. Grumio had suddenly grown shy again, awkward, and was looking down at the cobbled street.

'Have fun,' Marcus replied, keeping his expression free of any taunting, all the more effectively teasing his older brother. 'Learn a lot!'

'Watch out for the witch,' Bran added cheerfully.

'Witch?' Marcus asked, with Telemachus clearly wondering the same thing.

'Oh, my sister, Rhiannon. I believe you have both met her.' He rolled his eyes in a friendly, conspiratorial manner. He turned to Telemachus. 'She told me all about your encounter in the hills. It was high time someone put her in her place.'

Telemachus blushed scarlet. 'I didn't mean to ... I

mean, it wasn't intentional . . . I didn't know she was a girl or that the person I struck . . .'

'What? You struck a girl?' Marcus could not believe his ears.

'Forget it. I'll explain later. I've got to go now with Grumio,' Telemachus replied angrily.

Grumio looked relieved to be going, so the two set off at a fast pace.

Marcus and Bran stood watching them go. Marcus was pleasantly baffled; he'd get the story out of Telemachus that evening. Without needing to talk, he and Bran climbed the last bit of the slope to the granary. The building itself looked like all the other buildings in the fort, built of light-brown sandstone blocks, but it did have massively buttressed walls and a surprisingly thick stone roof. It also had steps at one end.

'Why the raised floor?' Bran asked Marcus, who was already busy looking for pebbles to toss at the terriers stretched out and panting in the building's shade.

'Because it's the granary. The floor's raised to allow air to circulate underneath,' he told him. 'Grain, vegetables and meat are all stored here, so the idea is to keep the place as dry as possible. The food stored here feeds the cohort for the whole winter. Come here. I'll show you!'

He ran around to the side of the building and crouched down by a long slit in the stone wall. He peered in and then beckoned Bran to do the same. Inside they could see little stone pillars spaced evenly under the granary floor. 'A perfect home for rats,' Marcus told his friend. 'The terriers catch and kill them. They're so small they can just get in through these slits. It'd be funny if a terrier ate so many rats he couldn't get back out,' he observed happily.

Bran looked disconcerted somehow.

'How do you store your grain, then?' Marcus asked, suddenly curious and a little surprised.

'We put it in raised buildings, like you, only they're woven birch and thatched, built on stilts. Sometimes we bury the grain in deep pits, which works too.' Bran was solemn now, keeping his face unreadable.

Marcus could see this, but didn't understand. So he just asked about the odd notion of storing grain in the ground. 'The water in the ground doesn't get to it and soak it?'

'No, not if you dig the pit out of the way of underground streams. Sinking the grain keeps it well away from rats and other animals. And if you're raided, your enemy doesn't know where your grain pits are,' he explained, casting a shy glance at Marcus.

Marcus caught the glance and understood. This was still a very new friendship and suddenly they were on tricky territory. To lighten the mood, he said, 'I bet I can hit that terrier, the one by the third slit there, just looking up at me. See it?' He focused steadily on the dog, waiting for Bran's answer.

'You can't hit that terrier. I bet your pebble flies into the slit instead.'

'What do you bet?'

There was silence from Bran, held long enough for Marcus to lose his concentration and look around at him.

Bran was looking up thoughtfully into the granary storage area at the line of thick columns running down the centre of the room.

'What do you bet, Bran?' Marcus pushed.

'This granary is a lot better built than our grain huts, Marcus. It holds much more and is so sturdy, I suppose it'll last forever. You don't have to worry about raids or even animals coming up. And the terriers take care of the rats.' He turned slowly to Marcus. 'I bet you a pair of my bronze horse harnesses that you can't hit that terrier.'

Marcus inhaled sharply. 'A pair of those harnesses? Bran! Those are really special, really beautiful. You don't want to wager them in a silly bet!' He looked closely at Bran to understand this odd behaviour. 'I bet you a fresh oyster!'

Both boys gave a laugh. It was a good bet. Bran had never eaten an oyster.

'Throw!' he commanded.

Marcus knew that face. A person cornered looked like that. He picked up a pebble, took aim and threw. The stone's trajectory was high, smooth and fast, but it bounced off the stone wall behind the terrier, causing the dog to perk up and stare alertly at Marcus, but not even to move. Both boys just walked on, as though nothing of interest had happened. Neither wanted to make the other feel bad.

SECRETS IN THE WOODS

Telemachus was having better luck than Bran. Grumio had led him out of the east end of the fort and down the cliff side to the northern plains. They'd walked up the long slope to the cluster of trees on the next ridge. Even just walking, Telemachus noticed that his steps rustled the long grass and left footprints in any soft soil whereas Grumio's were silent and invisible. Grumio didn't speak, which was a blessing to Telemachus. He did notice, though, that Grumio's face was alert, registering impressions, Telemachus guessed. But of what? Sounds? Sights? He couldn't imagine. Grumio had got quite a way ahead of Telemachus when suddenly Telemachus saw him leap forward and down. He rose, holding a hare. Telemachus was stunned. Then he saw Grumio stroke the hare, set it down and let it go.

Telemachus ran up to him. 'How did you do that?'

Grumio fixed his old eyes on Telemachus's fresh, eager face. 'Listen. Know the sound of every creature. Watch every movement.'

'But I can hardly hear above the sounds of my own footsteps. How do you walk so silently?' he demanded.

Grumio didn't answer but turned and walked on. Exasperated, Telemachus followed, but this time trying to hear and see everything. Without thinking about his steps, they grew quieter. Then Grumio froze, slowly turned his face to Telemachus and rolled his eyes over to the far right. Telemachus looked and there was a hare, pressed close against the ground, panting, its body quivering with its rapid pulse beat. Telemachus approached it in slow motion. He perspired as he willed his body to move ever so slowly towards the hare. He felt Grumio's eyes upon him and looked into his face to see a silent command: more slowly. Closer and closer he crept, moving so slowly he feared he might topple backwards. Then suddenly, in a single darting movement, he grabbed at the hare, then held it up triumphantly to Grumio. Grumio smiled and walked on into the woods. Telemachus tried to stroke the hare as Grumio had done, but it twisted and whirled and jumped about so violently in his grip that, alarmed, he let it go. The hare scampered away, but Telemachus felt good. He hurried after Grumio, not sure exactly in which direction he had gone.

Grumio had disappeared. Probably on purpose, Telemachus thought to himself. After fruitlessly searching for prints or signs, he began to retrace his steps. Eventually he heard a sound to his left and crept towards it, pushing through dense foliage. There, in a hidden culvert, surrounded by forest, stood Rhiannon, her red hair blazing in the direct sun. She too was motionless, but was holding a long sword perfectly upright and still, its scabbard directly before her face. Suddenly she raised the long sword, swung it down in a fierce swoop, then pulled it up again in a symmetrical curve, returning it to the starting position before her face. Telemachus was transfixed. Who *is* this girl? he wondered. How is it she can wield a sword almost the length of her own body? He watched her take a step and repeat the attack, now swinging the sword in the opposite arch. Then he felt a breath at the back of his neck. Grumio was less than a hand's breadth behind him. Telemachus had heard nothing. Suddenly, all he wanted was to get away from this world with its sword-swinging maidens and its ghostly guides; but he was keener still not to reveal his presence to Rhiannon and so obeyed Grumio's silent command to depart. By the time Telemachus had turned to follow, Grumio was already out of sight.

THE DYING GAUL

Back at Vercovicium Bran had a good idea. 'I remember when the auxiliaries were building the latrine. It'll be stinky there now, in summer, but you can play a great trick on the soldiers.' Bran was trying to lighten the atmosphere after the episode with the bet.

'Tricks like what?' Marcus asked, falling in with Bran. They walked around the granary on its northern side and headed straight on, past a huge barracks, with the east side of the fort's inner wall directly before them.

'Frogs! You will see.' Bran smiled.

'Frogs! Brilliant,' Marcus agreed.

'But first there's something else I want to show you.'

'How do you know this fort so well?' Marcus asked. He couldn't help feeling slightly jealous that Bran knew the fort – his own father's fort – better than he did.

Bran gave Marcus a wry, knowing smile. 'This is my fort.'

'What do you mean?' Marcus stood taller.

'I was only a toddler when the Romans started to build this fort. All my childhood everyone I knew talked about it and about what the land was like before the fort was here. It seems as if I can remember too. My tribe used to plough and plant straight along the slope of the cliff. I remember watching, from the hill opposite, rows of grain on the slope waving in the wind, looking like the sea. All the land we can see in all four directions from here is Brigantian land and has been for generations and generations. But for me, ever since I can remember, this land has been occupied by you Romans.'

Marcus looked directly at Bran. What was his point? And what was Marcus supposed to do about it anyway?

'You told me you liked to be with the soldiers, that they liked you. All that father–son talk . . .'

Now Bran could hear the rattle of menace in Marcus's tone. He sat himself down on the steep slope and then lay back on the cobblestones and dirt, looking up at the sky. Marcus felt foolish standing over him, so he too sat and then lay down, not looking at Bran.

'After Claudius conquered most of this island, you know that Queen Boudicca of the Iceni led a revolt against him and, despite a lot of damage, failed.'

'Yes,' Marcus answered evenly.

'We had a queen then too –'

Marcus interrupted. 'I know, Cartimandua.'

'Yes, and did you know she sided with the Romans? So for the past sixty years legionaries have been on Brigantian land.' Bran looked over at Marcus's face and saw he was about to explode with frustration. 'Marcus! You have no idea what it's like to be conquered. How *could* you know? You've spent your life in Rome, I imagine, and, though I've never seen it, everyone tells me it's gigantic and magnificent. All you've ever heard of is triumph. Romans rule the world. Here, we still think all the time of when we lost to you, and why, and how . . . It's confusing. I know my people chose to welcome in the Romans, and your Empire has brought us great benefits. My father died battling for the Romans. My life has been spent with them, and they've always been friendly, though serious.' He looked away, thinking. 'But my family has been harmed. You've seen Rhiannon's anger.'

Marcus stood silently. The sun shone brightly on them and clouds were scuttling across the immense sky. He saw crows, or maybe rooks, spinning against the blue.

'It's not just that the legionaries and auxiliaries were friendly. Marcus, I admire the Roman ways. That's the truth, even if I feel disloyal to my people in saying it. Your ways are better,' he said, looking Marcus straight in the face, his shoulders squared, as though expecting a blow from someone. 'Look at those surgical instruments! The granary, the bathhouse, the latrines! I'm not talking just from today. I've lived among Roman engineering all my life. Look at the roads, the forts, the Wall, the towns.' He grew red in the face. 'The trade network, ships, everyone speaking Latin,' he spat out. 'I . . . I don't know who I am. Just the son of a conquered man who helped the conquerors? A Brigante sounds best . . .'

Marcus hardly recognized Bran at that moment. He was leaning up on one elbow, looking at the ground, and seemed simultaneously haggard and proud, a whipped dog and a free man.

'Bran,' he began hesitantly, 'in Rome I once saw a copy of an ancient Greek statue made over three hundred years ago. It's of a dying Gaul who had bravely fought the Greeks. You – you remind me of him right now.'

'Who won?' Bran asked quietly.

Marcus dropped his eyes.

'Listen, Marcus, I know we're new friends, but, well, I do feel I can tell you that it isn't good being conquered.'

Marcus looked shyly at Bran. He had never had a 'conquered boy' speak to him on the subject of being conquered and it was embarrassing. Still, if we're to be friends, we have to have such talks, he thought.

'Bran –' he looked not shyly but more levelly at his new friend – 'yes, it's true that that Gaul was conquered, but the point is he was noble, and that's how the sculptor showed him. I mean, the losing side has heroes too. That's what my Greek tutor, Titus Helius, has been teaching me from *The Iliad*.'

Bran interrupted. 'What is *The Iliad*?'

Marcus couldn't hide his surprise. 'A poem about the Trojan War. You know, *The Iliad*, *The Odyssey* . . . Homer, *you* know . . .' His voice trailed off and now he blushed with embarrassment. 'You don't know. Well, how could you? You have to be taught, just like me,' he ended, baffled and embarrassed.

'Well, I haven't been, have I? I know a lot, but it's about farming and the land here, and the animals, about wool and weaving, and metalwork.' He had grown strangely calm. 'I've heard the conquered peoples of my land and those they call the Celts make the best metalwork in the world, better than anything the Romans or the Greeks can do.' He looked at Marcus, part in confidence, part questioningly.

'I've always heard that too,' Marcus quietly agreed. Then, after a moment, he said, 'Bran, teach me about the Brigantes.'

Bran looked surprised and sad, but then, picking up pace, said after a moment, 'All right. Here's a plan. I'd like to show you the ancient Brigantian meeting place near your fort Vinovia or maybe Morbium, halfway to Eboracum. It's miles from here, so our mothers wouldn't allow us to go. But I can get two horses and we can ride there, spend the night, and ride back before dinner the next day, and we could just say you're staying with me.' He looked at Marcus solemnly. 'Do you want to do that?'

Bran's plan, Marcus knew, directly contravened his father's orders to stay near the fort. But it was important to Bran and he didn't hesitate. 'Yes,' he said, giving back to Bran exactly the same direct look.

Bran glanced at him. 'All right. And you teach me about that poem.'

The two looked at each other and smiled.

FUTURE THOUGHTS

After Grumio left him at the Praetorium, Telemachus lay in his bed thinking about this extraordinary day. Rhiannon had undone him. He didn't want to think about her. He wanted to think about something else, about who he was, about his future. He hoped he might return to Rome, not exactly to get away from here – an involuntary vision of Rhiannon in the clearing, her red hair, rose before him – but perhaps to be apprenticed to his uncle, the Quaestor. Telemachus knew that, because of his Batavian father, he was only a member of the equestrian class, but that by becoming a quaestor he might be able to move upwards to become a procurator of a province and invited ('adlected', he remembered his father teaching him the word) into the Senate. And as my uncle only has daughters, my father says he would be pleased to help me, to carry on the hopes of the family. Memories of Rome – and visions of Rhiannon – swirled in his mind as he fell fast asleep.

Meanwhile, Rhiannon, tiring of her sword practice, wandered home. When she reached the Military Road she stopped and looked at it, at its paving stones, its camber, the ditches on either side and the earth mounded up beyond each ditch. She turned her head right and looked west along the road that was perfectly straight as far as her eye could see. She turned to look east and again the road stretched perfectly straight, again as far as her eye could see. She'd never actually stopped to think about the road before.

Where did it go? She looked east again. She knew it went to Coria, her market town, only a few miles away. Then she thought, does it go further? Of course it does, a voice in her head mocked. How much further? she heard the voice ask derisively. How much further? she teased herself. How much further? Imagine Eboracum, Londinium, a short boat trip and then Gaul. Now her eyes widened. She had never been to those places and found she couldn't imagine them. Her mother had relatives in Gaul and always said its countryside looked something like the Brigantian territory. Maybe Gaul does look like this, she mused, as she looked up and down the valley, then north and south at her settlement's hill and the cliff with the Wall, vallum and ditch winding their way across the horizon.

This was her land. I belong here, she said to herself. But her eyes came back to the road. For the first time she saw it not as part of the land but as apart from it. The stone of the road had been quarried from her hills. She glanced up the slope at Vercovicium and thought that that stone too had come from her hills, as had all the stone in all the forts and roads up and down this valley. With the stone of the conquered land they built roads, forts, towns. They took the land and imprisoned it in stone. Romans and stone. Power and stone.

What lay beyond Gaul? she asked herself. Why, Rome, of course, the little voice answered. And what is beyond Rome?

What is beyond Rome? This question terrified her, and suddenly she realized that she knew very little. She also realized, immediately and almost before thinking it, that she could not live her life in just one valley. She would have to discover what lay down and up that road. Then a vision of Telemachus floated into her head. She saw again his dark, curly hair and dark eyes. She saw his lean, muscular build. He is from Rome, the little voice whispered. He knows what Rome looks like. Rhiannon stood transfixed by the road of stone, lost in thought.

FROGS AND CUCUMBERS

Her brother and Marcus could not have been further from Rhiannon in mood and activity. Back at Vercovicium, they passed a barracks and Bran suddenly began smiling and said, 'We can see something here that was meant to bring good luck. It's something we share – Roman, Brigante, Greek and Gaul. You've got till I count to a hundred to find it.' With that, he shoved Marcus into the last room in the barracks block.

Marcus began looking for the 'good luck' thing that everyone shares. 'Give me some clues!'

'All right,' Bran agreed, still smiling. 'Correction: half the world has it.' He laughed, delighted. 'You're close to it now. Oops, now you're further away. Good, closer again.'

Marcus was stumbling around the barracks feeling foolish. There were four double bunk beds in there and, although it was tidy, the room was jammed with men's equipment and personal possessions. Marcus did not like being in there for no reason.

'Quick, Bran. Help me or we'll get caught!' This time it was a real wail.

'You give up?'

That angered Marcus. 'No.'

'All right.'

After more useless searching, Marcus turned to Bran. 'This had better be worth it. I give up.'

'Ha!' And with that, he walked over to the wall directly in front of him and traced, with his finger, the outline, carved into the stone, of a huge phallus, like a cucumber, with two rather small balls on either side of it. He turned with glee to see Marcus's reaction.

'What? Why is that there?'

'The auxiliaries told me it was done secretly, by one of the soldiers, to bring him luck.'

'How does carving a ... bring luck? If the centurion found out, would the soldier get in trouble?'

'The soldiers told me he'd get in trouble. That's why it's sort of hard to see, until you know where it is. As for the luck, all I can guess is that not to have one would be very bad luck indeed for a man – and to have one seems pretty basic.'

'Basic!' Marcus roared with laughter.

Bran burst out laughing too. Finally they felt carefree again, laughing at a dirty joke.

'The auxiliaries told me there are at least eight carved along the Wall!' Bran boasted.

'No! Have you found them?' Marcus asked enviously.

'No, but maybe we two could go looking! No one

would know what we were doing and we'd be under the watch of the guards, auxiliaries and legionaries the whole time!'

'What a great idea. I'll just tell my mother we're walking along the Wall. She can't object to that!'

So the two friends carried on happily, walking along the east side of the fort's wall, until they came to two stone cisterns, almost in the south-east corner of the fort. The boys looked at each other, not saying a word, and began searching the ground around the cisterns. Bran jumped first, on to the ground, cupped hands leading, and then stood, a look of delight and triumph on his face. Marcus's eyes followed Bran's movements and then he did the same. The two stood there, both with hands cupped, still not speaking. They looked around, then slowly walked over to the lower cistern.

Suddenly the sounds of men's voices, talking and laughing, broke their silence. Although as many as thirty men might use the latrine, only about ten seemed to be there now. The smell was obnoxious in summer as it rained less, making it harder to collect the water used to flush the waste away. The boys froze, then Bran gently placed his cupped hands at the opening where the stone trough from the upper cistern connected with the lower. Out of his hands a little frog jumped, right into the lower cistern. Marcus followed suit. The boys stood back with pleased, satisfied smiles on their faces.

'It'll take a while for them to swim through to the latrine,' Marcus gravely noted.

'But they'll get there,' Bran added.

'Yes. And the unlucky man who forgot to carve his symbol –' Marcus was sniggering now – 'may find himself washing his bum with a frog.'

'Pity!' Bran beamed with delight.

Both boys' grins grew wider as they heard yowls and curses from within the latrine. There was the sound of large animals – men – bashing into each other as they moved fast and awkwardly. Yes, the boys nodded. Good.

PART TWO

GHOSTLY DREAMS

All around Vercovicium, especially to the south, great trees waved their branches. Beech, birch, alder, willow, oak and hazel swayed in the strong late-summer winds. The noise they made was like laughter.

'Oh, stop it, Gurn!' issued a voice from a large ancient oak that waved around as if dancing. 'I'm not as young as I used to be.'

'You haven't aged a moment, dear queen,' the wind whispered.

The oak settled briefly and seemed almost to shake out her tangled branches like the folds of a gown. 'I do not seek compliments, as you well know. Three months have passed and what have you accomplished?'

The wind blew up again, pulling and turning the old oak. The tree twisted and creaked, but, because its roots were deep under the ground, it was not to be distracted by all this blowing about. 'You will remind the boy of his people's ancient ways. You will protect the coming child.'

'I will. The boy is brave; the parents of the unborn one have just barely become aware of his existence. I will visit the mother in a dream. She is beautiful and lonely,' the wind suspirated.

'Do not upset her, Gurn, I command you.' The wind whirled away, flipping the oak's leaves on to their pale sides.

4 EVERYTHING CHANGES

CLAUDIA AND GAIUS

The boys had finished eating one evening, leaving their parents to linger over the fruit, sweet cakes and wine. Claudia glanced at Gaius as she nodded to the slave to pour her more wine. She could see his mood was, as usual, distracted.

'That will be all,' he spoke to the slaves, indicating that they could now depart for the evening.

'Gaius,' she said, slowly turning her head, showing to full advantage her beautiful neck and upswept hair, 'we've been here nearly a full season and still you remain wrapped in your bachelor habits.'

He smiled, aware of her tricks and flirting ways. 'Bachelor habits? Do you mean the sort shown on Greek vases of wild drinking and dancing slave girls? I would hope I might remember that.'

'Well, I'm not surprised, you're so absorbed in your work! You could be surrounded by the loveliest Nubian maidens and not notice. I've been here long enough to see that, although there is much to think about in running this fort, there haven't been battles, much less skirmishes. What is it that so occupies you?' She was still smiling, but there was a warning note in her words and Gaius heard it.

He slid off his couch, walked around to her, approaching from behind, and kissed her neck, something he knew she liked. 'My darling, has it occurred to you that there haven't been any skirmishes precisely because I am so vigilant?' His face darkened and he seemed about to speak, but stopped. As her back was to him, she didn't see this. 'And allow me to say that I am not maintaining bachelor habits, quite the reverse. Having you here these past three months has been wonderful.'

He couldn't see her face, but assumed she was pleased and smiling, which wasn't necessarily so. As he was returning to his couch, his mind was already on his constant worry: military strategy. There had, in fact, been recent reports of tribal activity north of the Wall. Men were gathering at night, then dispersing. Fort Blatobulgium, in Brigantian territory once claimed by the Novantae and Selgovae, had had numerous sightings.

She watched him sink back into his own thoughts and decided to recall him. 'Gaius, let us talk.'

'About what, my dear?'

'Oh, about Brigit, about Grumio, about the future –'

'Ah, may I choose among those topics?'

'You may.'

'Brigit first. I think she seems to be quite useful to you. Is this true?'

'Yes, but she is odd.'

'How so?'

'She seems scared often, for no reason. Nervous.'

Claudia could see Gaius was already bored. 'Let us talk about Grumio. Tell me what your history is with him, why you value him.'

'Claudia, I have a lot of work still to do tonight. These are not important topics.'

'Then let us talk about the future. Gaius,' Claudia said in a challenging tone, 'I am concerned about both boys. Telemachus has missed his *toga virilis* ceremony two years running. When are you going to help him through that? Are his sessions with Grumio meant to compensate? And Marcus worries me. He's been a bit peculiar since we've come to Britannia –'

'Anything else?' he replied drily.

'Yes. Us. You say it has been "wonderful" to have me here. You know I am going to have a baby, Gaius. What is our future? Do we stay here and raise the baby? For how long? Do we return to Rome or go somewhere else?'

He lay back on his couch, poured himself some wine and took a sip before answering her. 'Claudia ...' He paused for a second and she knew he was irritated. 'I'm glad you and the boys are here. This has been a very pleasant summer, made so by your presence. You are now with child and that will enliven our springtime. I hope you are happy and I believe the boys are reasonably so.'

'Will we be raising this baby at Vercovicium?' she repeated.

'You have married a military man and you know the drill. I will serve here until I am promoted or returned permanently to civil life. If promoted, I hope to command an *ala milliaria*, of which there is only one in all Britannia. If successful, I would probably be sent to another province. We may go back to Rome, if I am assigned a good civil service job. If returned to civil life, anything could happen. Stay with me if you like or return to Rome.'

'"If you like"! What would *you* like?'

He rose and looked at her briefly. 'We may discuss these things some other time. I am meeting Quintus now.'

Claudia looked steadily at him. She understood he had terminated the conversation.

'Tomorrow I hope to visit Coria with Brigit,' she said. 'We've only been once and that was over a month ago. Marcus is spending the day and night with Bran. I think Telemachus may go adventuring. He has been studying hard.' Her voice was neutral and distant.

He had turned to leave the room while listening to her and now he swung round abruptly. 'Both boys and you away from Vercovicium tomorrow?' His irritation was spilling over into a new area.

She caught his drift. 'We know the situation with the northern tribes.' She spoke with firmness and a hint of condescension.

You do not know the situation, as I have carefully kept it from you, he mentally responded.

'Each of us will be careful,' she continued. 'I am with Brigit, Marcus with Bran, and Telemachus plans, I think, to visit the building site of Brocolitia, staying close to the Wall.' Irritating, she thought. How foolish does he think we are? Her body twitched on the couch with suppressed anger.

He saw the movement and read it correctly. 'This is barbarian territory, even if it used to be that of our allies, the Brigantes. It is not civilized. Rebellions are possible everywhere. You don't know everything, Claudia. Only our vigilance and superior military power hold them in check. You three are lambs among wolves.'

'We know that! You give us no credit, no credit at all.'

'I just don't know what each of you is doing.'

'What do you think we're doing?'

'I don't know. I know why I'm here, what my job is. But . . .'

'Gaius, we have been here three months and you and I have not had one day together.' She tried hard to compose her face into an attractive expression, to keep out the irritation. 'Could we not go out? See some of the countryside together?'

'See some of the countryside together?' he parroted, incredulous. 'Do you recall where we are living, why we're here?'

She rushed on. 'We might spend a few days travelling. We could visit Eboracum and meet with friends. Or go to Lindum, or Deva –' her voice was beginning to rise now – 'or even Londinium! Why can't we go somewhere together that is amusing and interesting? We could go to the amphitheatre, perhaps see some races. I would love to visit Verulamium and Camulodunum. Or how about a huge excursion to Aquae Sulis? Everyone says the waters there completely revive a person.'

'Claudia, I have no time for such "excursions".'

'Really, Gaius! There must be *something* for me to do, beyond gardening with Grumio and cooking with Brigit.'

Finally she stopped talking. Gaius just looked at her in silence. He sighed and walked towards the door. 'I understand next spring a new prefect is coming to Vindolanda with his wife. That will be someone for you to get to know.'

'Don't you want to spend time alone with me?' she asked quietly.

'We spend every dinner and night together.'

'Yes,' she agreed, adjusting her position on the couch. 'But I don't have your attention, nor do the boys. And I am concerned in different ways about each one. Telemachus also needs more to do up here. The tutoring, the sessions with Grumio and the exercising with the auxiliaries aren't enough. He needs tuition in becoming a man. This is one of the main reasons we came,' she said, looking directly into his face, trying at once to reach, insult and convince him. 'And Marcus . . .' She paused. 'Marcus is probably all right, as long as he has Bran, but I do think he would benefit from spending more time with you – as we all would.'

Gaius stood at the door now, but he had stopped to listen to her remarks on the boys. It was true, he probably did need to attend to them more. He glanced at her belly and was reassured that soon she would be preoccupied with the pregnancy and would forget this talk of excursions. So much to do, he thought, as the issues he would discuss with Quintus swarmed back into his mind, colliding with this new concern about the boys.

Claudia saw how tired he was, and troubled. She sighed.

He was her only escape, entertainment, social equal here. He was the only one who could help give the boys what they needed. He was everything to them, and commander of the biggest fort along the Wall in perilous times. She looked down at her plate and said nothing more. He left the room to meet Quintus.

THE SACRED PLACE

In the time since the family had first come to Vercovicium, their life at the fort had fallen into familiar patterns, but, as Claudia had told Gaius, Telemachus was restless to get out and see the countryside and maybe meet someone – anyone. He decided to go for a long walk alone. He'd been following a strict routine for three months now and felt increasingly rebellious. Every day he met with his Greek tutor, Titus Helius, for four hours. They translated Homer, Plato, Sophocles and Aristotle. They read the poetry of Virgil and the history of Livy. His father had recently begun to check on them daily and Telemachus could see he took pride in his son's ability to recite these works from memory. After lunch, he was allowed to join the legionaries and auxiliaries as they practised in the exercise court. Although marching was tedious, the testudo was exciting. Every man played his part, his shield locked with that of the man ahead, to create a giant impenetrable shield to stop attack from above. He had perfected the jabbing motion of the sword and the throwing of the javelin. The soldiers didn't mind his being there; there was always need of an extra person to spar with, or make a wall with, or retrieve the *hastati* or javelin. For him, best of all was how his muscles had grown and hardened. His physique had changed from a boy's to a man's in this short time at Vercovicium.

Somewhat surprisingly, he had come to know and respect Grumio too. The old man had proved in their many sessions together to be a brilliant scout. They had not seen Rhiannon again, though anticipating finding her had brought great improvements in Telemachus's ability to walk silently and listen for every sound. He understood that this training was different from the military practice he did with the auxiliaries, and very different from the requirements of the *toga virilis* ceremony, yet it was having a profound effect upon him.

As for Grumio, he was delighted with their expeditions. It was good to lope across the land again, on the prowl. And taking this cub with him was interesting. He nodded to himself. He knew what this meant to the Prefect. They understood each other. He also understood about the girl – more than Telemachus, he often smiled to himself.

Evenings for Telemachus were spent memorizing his authors, but sometimes discussing the Wall with his father. That was his happiest time. He understood much more now what his father had to consider and what his hopes were. He'd grown a lot less impatient and had taken on a longer view: that true conquering comes from cooperation with – and the regular collection of taxes from – the local people. He knew his more mature attitude and greater knowledge were pleasing his father and hoped that one day soon Gaius would remember he still hadn't had his *toga virilis* ceremony.

Such hopes sustained him, but today he wanted to cut loose and wander about the countryside. He'd hardly had any time to do this, unlike Marcus, who had been allowed to go off with Bran whenever he wanted. True, Marcus had to spend two hours every day with Titus Helius, and sometimes worked out in the yard, but mostly he disappeared into the folds of the hills with his friend.

Telemachus decided to find the new well where, he'd heard, the auxiliaries had begun to worship Coventina. He knew she could be worshipped at any spring or pool but that the well near Brocolitia that was still being built was talked about among the soldiers as a newly discovered source of the divinity. The well was about eight miles away. Telemachus decided to hop on a supplies cart travelling along the track. As this track served all sixteen forts and their *vici*, it was heavy with traffic, mostly military. He would have no trouble getting a ride. His curiosity about Coventina had started on the parade ground, where the Nervii and auxiliaries from Gaul talked of the goddess and planned devotional visits. They spoke of her as their protector, a healer and even a guide to the Otherworld. With a shiver, Telemachus remembered one Celt solemnly explaining how he was going to toss his sandals into the well to ease his passage after death.

The road went straight down the valley that separated the dark basalt cliff from the heavily wooded, southern hills. He felt safe and protected within this valley, but was sorry not to be able to see, because of the valley's enclosure, the magnificent view from the top of the cliff ridge. Nor could he see the ditch dug beyond the north side of the Wall. Still, the road allowed a close study of the vallum ditch, which many thought was even more impressive than the Wall. Amazing construction, he mused, looking right and left at the continuous earthworks and finally the Wall, snaking themselves over the countryside. I want to follow them as far as I can see, he thought, up and down, over the horizon. The earthworks mesmerized him.

Just before the cart reached the construction site that would be Brocolitia, he jumped off and followed the pilgrims. He knew there was a temple to Mithras too; many of these men might be going there. Ever since he was a little boy, he had wanted to become a worshipper of Mithras. Only men – they were mostly soldiers – could belong and membership was a sign of masculinity, honour and discipline. I wonder if my father is a member, he thought, knowing that membership was secret.

Most of the men walking in front of him followed the path to the right and went around the hill to the temple that was nestled in a hollow in a rolling landscape. Telemachus glanced over. It was a squat, stone building of one room, without windows, built right next to fort Brocolitia. Only members could enter and its entry was ferociously guarded, he knew. Pine-cone-smelling smoke rose from a low chimney at its front end. He could hear the rumbling of prayers as the men chanted in unison under its low, dim vault. Darkness, blood and courage were central to its secret ritual. He heard a cockerel screech, then silence, then a burst of chanting. He couldn't make out the words, but felt their mysterious intensity and the cult's privacy. He turned north, facing the Wall, and began to follow the Coventina worshippers up the incline to the water source.

A few of the soldiers walked ahead of him, crossing through the vallum on a causeway and then entering the curious structure of a walled room with no roof. Telemachus slipped in behind them. The walls enclosed the well, presenting it as a sacred basin. The men circled the well and stood quietly, looking intent. Telemachus could see that the well was of Roman construction. He'd been told that when the legionaries began to build the vallum, ditch and then Brocolitia, they saw that the ground, even so high up on the basalt cliff, was spongy and waterlogged. The legionary engineers found the water source and, feeding lead pipes into the ground, led the water down the slope, away from the construction, and enclosed the 'well'. Overnight, auxiliaries began to speak about this magic well, looking to it as yet another place to commune with Coventina.

As he watched, the soldiers prayed silently, then, one by one, threw into the well some small object, like a rectangular bronze plaque, maybe a trinket, even bits of glass and leather. He knew each object represented some worry – over health or welfare or family or the battles ahead. He looked into the anxious weathered face of a burly man whose dirty blond hair hung about his furrowed, fleshy forehead. From Raetia or the Rhineland, he thought. Standing next to that man was a short, wiry soldier with darkly tanned skin whose nervous, angry eyes made him ill at ease. He could be from as far away as Tarraconesis or even Narbonne, he thought with surprise. This goddess has a vast territory and must be powerful. Telemachus began to sense her presence here by the Wall and felt guilty spying on her rites.

I am out of place here, he thought, and not doing Coventina proper service. I'd rather seek her in some shady, private spot. So he turned and walked down the incline, over the road and up the opposite hill, into the woods. After reaching the crest, he looked down and saw the river curling around the hill's southern flank. Slipping and sliding, he soon reached it.

There, at the bottom of the hill, just away from the river, stood a pool made by an eddy, surrounded by ash and silver birches. It looked like the floor of a magnificent temple and the trees were like columns. He followed his fancy and imagined a mosaic of Coventina, or maybe Minerva, covering the floor. 'I have heard of the beautiful baths dedicated to Sulis Minerva, somewhere far west of the provincial capital. Maybe we could dedicate this to her, healing goddess of legionaries and auxiliaries,' he murmured, leaning dreamily against an ash. As he leaned, he focused on the ash's winged seeds, clustered, brown, still hanging on the tree. Those ash keys would fall in spring, he knew. He used to love trying to catch them as they whirled frantically to the ground. Now he remembered what he'd been studying with Titus Helius only a few days ago, how Achilles says:

Of the earth this, the upper limit, is seen at our feet
next to the air; but below, it proceeds to infinity.

He felt clever and adult reciting Achilles' lines from *The Iliad*. It was pleasing to be mature enough to contemplate death. His thoughts ran on: but the earth is here and does catch us all, all living things, and is our final resting place. He paused: but there again, I'm not afraid of dying.

In fact, the thought of death filled him with a warm and patriotic sense of his future glory. I will do brave and heroic acts for the Caesar Trajan Hadrian Augustus. Just thinking about his fine future made Telemachus move away from his ash and pose valiantly by the now deserted pool. He could see, in his mind's eye, an altar given and dedicated by him, making his vow to the Emperor:

IMP CAES TRAIANO HADRIAN AUG
TELEMACHUS AURELIUS RUFINUS
V S L M

Solemnly, in his deepest voice, he chanted over the pool, 'For the Emperor Caesar Trajan Hadrian Augustus, Telemachus Aurelius Rufinus willingly and deservedly fulfilled his vow.'

A girl's giggle cut through the air, horrifying Telemachus and shrivelling all the glory out of him. White-faced, he turned. There, hiding among the long limbs of the silver birches, was Rhiannon, doubled over in laughter. Her red hair seemed to fill the grove.

'Telemachus Aurelius Rufinus, you scare me!' she said as she smiled brightly up at him.

'I was praying to Coventina,' he spluttered indignantly.

'You were not,' she retorted, outraged that her goddess could be so abused. 'You were praying to Telemachus! And a lot of good that will do.' She burst into laughter again.

'Leave me! This is a private place.'

'*Again* you are telling me to leave you. I've seen you twice and twice you've ordered me to leave you. And this is a private place. It is my sacred place where you have no business being. I worship Coventina here and she is my patron deity. Now I am telling *you* to leave!'

Telemachus cocked his head and looked at her. She had no idea, of course, that he had seen her in the woods. She must not find out, he thought. 'Your patron deity? I thought she was a Celtic goddess, from the lands over the sea, not a goddess of Britannia.' His tone was different; it was calmer with a hint of genuine curiosity.

Now Rhiannon tucked down her chin while warily watching. 'What do you mean, a Celtic goddess?'

Telemachus raised his eyebrows and shrugged, slightly turning away from the conversation. 'That's what I learned from the auxiliaries at Vercovicium. They told me about her and how their people worship her.'

Rhiannon frowned and looked down. This was confusing. 'My father brought me up to worship her,' she insisted, raising her chin. 'As far as I am concerned, she is our deity and my patron goddess.' Then she remembered the road. Had worship of Coventina travelled to her valley along that road? Her eyes flashed a warning at Telemachus. 'She encourages me. She soothes me and promises me that you and your sort will one day leave our land.' Her voice suddenly seemed quiet, not fiery and confident. Hating the Romans came more easily than hating this particular Roman.

'Oh, well,' Telemachus began diffidently, 'there's no problem if many people worship her. And I suppose one day we will leave, but I can't imagine when. Our Empire has been gathering lands for six hundred years and hasn't left one yet. Anyway, how do you know Coventina encourages you? And as auxiliaries pray to her too, do you think they are praying for her to help them leave Britannia? No, they're praying for victory against your neighbours.' Although his point was harsh, his tone was still tentative and conciliatory. He couldn't stop looking at her hair. It dazzled him and made him forget what he was saying and even his mood. He thought of her with the sword, thrusting it high, swirling it down. This delicate girl.

Rhiannon was clearly listening hard to what he was saying, and studying him. 'The auxiliaries pray to her to give them victory over the Novantae and Selgovae?'

'I think so. That would make sense. Those tribes are the enemy.' He watched her closely.

'So I am praying to her to make you leave and you are praying to her to give you more victories and more land.'

Telemachus turned his head and rubbed his neck. Without understanding all that was going on, he knew somehow it was about to be amusing. And he knew she knew too. He smiled but kept his face turned down. He felt her gathering her forces for another attack.

'I know she encourages me because I feel so much better after praying to her and giving her a votive offering,' she declared defiantly. Her tone was again confident but a little bewildered too. 'Yesterday I gave her two slender gold rings. Right here in this pool. I've always prayed to her. Don't you realize she is here and receives our gifts? She is a water goddess, a healer. She protects all who worship her.' Suddenly her face brightened as she saw how to make sense of these new confusions. 'She doesn't "take sides" in our wars! She loves and helps all who trust in her.' Her voice dropped to a whisper. 'She helps ease the pain and lone-liness I feel for my dead father.' Rhiannon looked away and flushed with anger at herself. Here she was seriously explaining her deepest faith and sorrow – to a Roman boy! Yet it felt right. It was right, for curiously, she realized, she actually liked him.

Telemachus now felt embarrassment. Her flushed face transfixed him. He instinctively knew not to comment on anything she had just revealed. 'You're right. I shouldn't be here, as I wasn't praying to her. But when I got here I started thinking about the earth and dying, and then –' he reddened – 'as you know, my vow . . .'

Rhiannon came out from behind the birches and sat on a fallen ash trunk near the pool. She had been coming here all her life and felt as much at ease here as by her mother's fire. But today the pool felt charged somehow, unsafe and exciting. 'Well, if you're thinking about falling ill, Coventina is the best goddess to pray to. She will protect you from all evils.' Rhiannon told herself that the goddess's kindness to everyone explained her growing tenderness. She looked up at Telemachus as she spoke, then slid over, just a bit, on the trunk.

Her woollen dress blended with the scenery and Telemachus thought she could have been wearing leaves and patches of sky. He liked the gleam of her bronze bracelet against her skin. As she slid over, her dress pulled against her side. Such a small waist! he thought. Then he frowned. Looking quickly into her face, he came over and sat, a little awkwardly, at the far end of the trunk. As her head was turned from him, the beads seemed to flash like fire.

'Who do you pray to, then? To the Emperor?' she asked.

'No! He expressly forbids that. I worship the deified emperors who came before him and I pray that the virtues of all our emperors may be visited upon our Emperor Hadrian.' He looked right at her for a second but quickly turned away, for it felt as though he was staring directly at the sun.

'Do you not pray to a deity? How do you thank the sky for its warmth and brilliance and the rain for making the crops grow? How do you thank the earth for seed and for holding us when we die? You can't thank deceased emperors for that!'

Telemachus sat stupidly gazing at her and thought, I know she's getting angry, I can tell the signs from when

Mother gets angry. But she is so beautiful! I've never met anyone like her. And with that thought, he slumped on the tree trunk and stared forlornly into space.

'Well?' she pushed.

'Well, what?' he answered stupidly.

'Do you not pray to a deity?' she persisted.

'Yes, as a matter of fact, I do,' he answered stoutly, if a little peevishly. 'Vesta is our household god. She is my mother's favourite because Vesta protects women and the family. My father likes Vesta because she stands for the eternal power and glory of Rome. He likes that she has the sacred fire burning day and night in her temple in the Forum Romanum. But my brother and I, together, prayed to Vesta to . . .' He faltered and grew shy.

'What? I won't laugh,' she said seriously, suddenly keenly aware of his embarrassment.

'Well, to bring our family back together again. You see, my father was away in Dacia for ten years. Oh, he came back sometimes on leave. But it wasn't the same. My mother and my grandmother raised us,' he concluded with a slight thrust of his chin. This was getting close to the bone. He hardly admitted such thoughts to himself, much less to anyone else.

Rhiannon's eyes grew round and dark. 'I understand. My father died when I was five, so my mother raised us too. No amount of offerings or prayers would bring him back. I . . . I am always angry about it. I hate the Romans for enlisting him, the Brigantes for – oh, everybody, for taking him. And I won't stop hating!' She glared at Telemachus.

He shrugged his shoulders and looked away. She seemed now wrapped in her thoughts.

'I don't want a life like my mother's, accepting her fate, weaving away, doing the best she can.' Rhiannon's face flushed for shame at her disloyalty. 'And I won't be like Brigit, pretending to be Roman –'

'She really is Roman, isn't she? I mean, she was born and raised in Rome,' he interrupted shyly.

'Oh, I know. Yes, but somehow she doesn't seem settled – in herself, I mean. She wants to be one of us and one of you. I don't want any of that. I am a Brigante but I don't want a Brigante's life! Or a shopkeeper's or a townswoman's. And keep me away from any soldiers! Maybe I could be a priestess . . .' Her voice trailed off.

'A priestess? Never.'

'Why not?' she asked quickly, and then, seeing his face, blushed deeply and looked away. 'I could, though. I could worship Coventina.' She turned to look at Telemachus. 'I know a little about Vesta. She did hear your prayers and did bring you together. I've heard she is a powerful household protector. Well, Coventina is known for protecting women, especially in childbirth. She heals all sorts of illnesses and worries. Maybe you could worship her too, along with Vesta. You could bring your family here to this pool – or to her well by the Wall.'

'My father would not allow it,' Telemachus said, an edge of bitterness in his voice. 'Even though he himself is a Batavian, he wouldn't go near this barbarian deity. I told you, he dedicates himself to the glory of Rome, not to healing.' He suddenly felt angry with his father, but didn't understand why. Was he different? After all, he thought, I myself believe in the glory of Rome. Only a moment ago I was promising to 'willingly and deservedly fulfil my vow' to Hadrian. What has got into me?

Rhiannon slid off the tree trunk and walked a bit away, towards the pool. He kept looking into the mud by his feet.

Suddenly aware of the heavy silence, Telemachus spoke: 'I hope to return to Rome, to be apprenticed under my uncle, who is a quaestor, a magistrate. I . . . I have lots of hopes after that, if I do well.'

She looked at him. 'Return to Rome? Do you want to?'

He looked at her and could not answer. She saw and returned the look.

'Well,' she said, 'my future affects my whole family. If I marry, my marriage will be seen as an alliance between my clan and my husband's. I will be linking my people to his. I can't just act on my own. And, the more I think about it,' she said, beginning gently to bang her clenched fists together, 'the more I worry about it.'

'Do you want to marry a Brigante or a Novantian or . . .' His voice trailed off. He looked at her. There was absolute silence.

She lifted her chin and looked straight at him. 'I'll tell you what I want. I want to know where the Military Road leads.'

He burst out laughing. 'The Military Road?' This was hardly the answer he was expecting.

She did not enjoy his laughter. 'Yes. What is the future

I have here? My mother, everyone, warns, "Be careful of boys. They'll take you up the hill and behind the Wall." What kind of a future is that?' She looked earnestly into his eyes, but he was now having even more trouble keeping a straight face.

She saw that his eyes sparkled with amusement and she began to giggle.

'At least that's good advice,' he said, laughing.

'Yes.' She smiled. 'And it's true.'

They both laughed.

When she looked at him now, he seemed to her like one of those noble Roman statues she'd seen at Eboracum. She saw how well proportioned his head, neck and shoulders were. He was very strong. Her glance slid down his body to his legs. Hard muscles showed beneath his woollen tunic. Suddenly their eyes met. Telemachus held her gaze for a few moments, but she looked away.

'I've got to go . . .'

'It will be dark soon . . .'

They both began speaking at the same time. Laughter. Ease. Glances again. Smiles. Both turned, saying no more, and went their opposite ways. Telemachus headed north, up the hill. Rhiannon simultaneously turned south, to find the river crossing towards home.

CARTIMANDUA'S FORTIFICATION

On the day that Telemachus decided to seek out Coventina, Marcus and Bran carried out their plot. Marcus got his mother's permission to pass the night at Bran's, and Bran got his mother's permission to pass the night with Marcus, somewhere in the countryside near Bran's settlement. But, as suspected by Modron, what both boys really planned was to ride down to the ancient Brigantian fortification, thirty miles south of the Wall.

'On horses we should get there in half a day,' Bran assured Marcus. 'Then we can look all around – it's huge – and we can sleep in the ruins of the queen's house.'

'The queen's house! Could we? Really? No one would mind?' Marcus couldn't believe such a wonderful plan.

'No, hardly anyone's there any more. It's tumbled down now and only a few farmers still live in some of the outbuildings. But there's a lot to see. The ditches and ramparts and vast open spaces just make you want to run,' he boasted.

He knew this tribal fortification had been the grandest in the north. It was the central place through which goods had been funnelled south to the tribes and the Romans, and north to the Selgovae and the Votadini. His had been the most important tribe of the north then, and that wasn't so long ago.

Marcus knew that neither his mother nor his father would approve of the plan. The distance was too great and, although the Brigantes supported the Roman presence, many of the tribes just north of the Wall did not and therefore even the Brigantian region was tense. Still, who notices twelve-year-old boys? he thought. Old enough to look after themselves, but too young to be soldiers or spies. 'At least that's what most adults think,' Marcus said to an agreeing Bran. So they concocted their plan, which should have worked. Marcus left Vercovicium just before Telemachus did. That way his parents stayed focused on his older brother. He ran through the *vicus*, over the causeway that cut through the vallum and ditch, across the cart road and up into the hills.

Meanwhile, Bran had been getting two horses, Cigfa and Cu, ready. They were small, hardy ponies, barely taller than he was, but standing behind him they looked huge. Their exhalation filled the air around Bran with steam. Marcus remembered how Bran had looked walking through the smoke of the *vicus*, and thought again how he and now his horses too seemed to be rising from the Otherworld. He scowled, trying not to think of the ghostly figures he had been seeing all summer. They would just appear a field or two away from him. But they don't hurt me, he thought. They don't even scare me. They just watch. Farmers, women and children in old-fashioned dark clothes, walking parallel to me, watching. They make me sad. His heart tightened and misery flowed into him. Suddenly he doubted the wisdom of going to Cartimandua's fortifications and whispered a prayer to Vesta.

He was also worried that his mother would find out and was terrified of what his father would say. Being the Prefect's son meant that he should know better than to disobey and that he could seriously compromise his father. What if that tattooed warrior shows up again and eats me, or turns me to stone, or changes me into a crow? he

109

thought. What if all those crows on the Wall are magically transformed legionaries and auxiliaries killed in battle? No, I'm just remembering my lessons. That's Odysseus's men magically altered by Circe. Maybe I need a mola plant to keep me safe, he tried to joke with himself. But he felt terrible.

Bran saw his friend's worried expression. 'What is it, Marcus?'

'Bran.' Marcus squarely faced Bran. 'Bran,' he repeated steadily.

Bran knew his friend well enough not to laugh or rush him. Something serious was about to be declared. He just stood there, holding the two bridles, looking back at Marcus and saying nothing.

'Bran, since I have come to north Britannia, I keep seeing figures, lots of them, in the distance, ploughing, sowing, planting. They never try to hurt me, but they make me sad. The problem is, no one else sees them. I point them out to Telemachus, or my mother, but they only see landscape. The day we first arrived, right near Vercovicium, I think I saw a spirit – a special one, a warrior.'

Bran looked very solemn and listened.

'This man, his torso was naked but tattooed with blue swirls. He had a moustache and his hair was filled with some sort of white powder that made it stand straight up. He had a gold torc around his neck, and –'

'Stop, Marcus. Stop,' Bran whispered. 'I know who you mean.'

'You do?' Marcus whispered back.

Bran nodded and pursed his lips. He shifted his eyes sideways while patting Cigfa's neck. He said quietly, 'I don't know what to say about the farmers. I have heard that some people can see spirits.' His eyes were worried as they looked at Marcus. He now looked away, shrugging. 'As for the warrior, even if you did see him, they say he doesn't care about children, even Roman ones. He wants the legions and auxiliaries to leave north Britannia.'

Startled, Marcus looked deep into his friend's face. 'You speak calmly of him, as if he didn't scare you. Bran, this is a spirit! I may be seeing scores of spirits! Tell me the truth. Tell me what you know. Please.'

Bran walked away a little from Marcus and wouldn't look at him. He rubbed the hair on top of his head and then squeezed himself with both arms. The only sound was the horses' noisy breathing and the stomping of their feet on the spongy ground. The early-morning mists shrouded them and kept even these sounds muffled.

'You are my friend, so I will tell you what I know.' He paused to let the solemnity of the confidence register on Marcus. 'I must first tell you a story. Queen Cartimandua had always supported the Romans and she established the north–south trade route that made our tribe so rich and important.'

'Bran, what has this to do with these spirits I keep seeing? You told me about her before,' he added crossly.

'I don't know about those spirits, Marcus. I have heard people talking about the warrior. His name is Gurn. They say he is the Spirit of the North.'

'Is that bad?' Marcus asked.

Bran smiled at his friend. 'That depends, I think. What would the Spirit of the North want? Building a huge, thick wall straight across his territory might not be it.'

Marcus nodded, looking down.

'All the tribes honour him: Brigantes, Novantae, Selgovae, Votadini, Dumnonii, even the Caledonians.' He paused for a moment. 'And he isn't alone.'

Marcus's head shot up.

'They say he is accompanied by the queen.'

'All right. Tell me her story.' Marcus spoke more patiently now.

'Her husband, Venutius, never did support the Romans, and some members of the tribe agreed with him. One day Cartimandua announced that she did not consider herself married to Venutius any longer and would now become the wife of one of her captains, a man named Vellocatus. I don't know if Venutius loved her or was jealous or ashamed, or just used this split as an excuse, but anyway he then gathered all the rebellious Brigantes and members of other tribes – like the Selgovae and the Novantae – and led a rebellion against Cartimandua. They seized her throne and she only escaped because the Romans rescued her. But then the Ninth Legion entered and retook the Brigantian lands. The Brigantes accepted the Roman presence and timber forts were built and roads cut into the land. Over the next sixty years, the forts were rebuilt in stone and the Wall, with its forts and defences, was put up.'

'What happened to Cartimandua and Venutius and . . .

what was his name?' Marcus asked, frowning to follow such a complicated story.

'Vellocatus. I don't really know. My mother told me she heard that Venutius escaped and hid in the mountains in the west, in his original lands. Maybe Cartimandua and Vellocatus went there too, or maybe she lived quietly in one of our farming settlements near the east coast. People say –' he paused now and looked about hesitantly – 'that they still hold some power.'

'What sort of power? Surely they must be dead?' Marcus asked, squinting at Bran in his effort to understand.

Bran stroked Cigfa's neck, ignoring the question for a moment. 'I don't know,' he whispered reluctantly.

'All right, Bran,' Marcus said quietly. 'But what about Gurn?'

Bran grew still and lowered his voice. 'Some say that deep in the Brigantes' hearts there is a spirit. Gurn, the Spirit of the North. It resists the Romans and inspires the northern tribes to rise up.'

'But Cartimandua supported the Romans. It doesn't make any sense that she and he would be in alliance. Anyway, do you think it's true?' Marcus hesitantly challenged. 'I have seen Brigantes around here and along the road to Eboracum, and they don't look rebellious to me. They look pleased and busy and at peace with the Roman ways and benefits.' Marcus frowned, but was aware of a petulance in his tone.

'I don't know, Marcus, I don't know. You've seen Gurn.' He looked quickly at his friend, curiosity but also deep envy in his eyes. 'I have heard rumours of other people having seen him. Maybe he exists, maybe he doesn't. But if he does exist, no one has said that he hurts people or frightens children. If he exists, we know what he wants. He wants the Romans and the auxiliaries out of northern Britannia. That's it.'

'Then who are those other spirits, the farmers?'

'I don't know, Marcus. If they are with Gurn, perhaps they are Britons of the past, his spirits. Maybe they're all the people who have lived on this land.' Exhaustion pulled Bran down, against Cigfa. He knew his explanation raised more questions than it answered. If there were spirits walking the land, Bran's homeland, why didn't Bran see them too? Why did his Roman friend see Gurn? He tried to draw comfort from Cigfa's pulse beating against his cheek. Finally, he asked quietly, 'Marcus, do you want to go to Cartimandua's fortifications?'

Marcus frowned. Now it was his turn to look away, to avoid Bran's eyes. Deep down, he knew one way Gurn could give the Roman authorities trouble was by interfering with the Prefect's son. But I want to see this famous fortification, he repeated to himself, I really do. We'll only be gone a day and a half. No one will know. He turned to Bran with a determined smile.

'All right,' Bran responded, smiling too, and turning immediately to the horses. 'These horses are about the same. They're frisky because they haven't been out today, but they'll settle down.'

Marcus took the reins, flung himself up on top of the

114

horse and, to his relief, landed plop in the middle of a familiar Roman, four-pommel saddle. He gathered in the reins, relaxed his legs and sat up straight, chin down. Bran mounted his horse, and they wheeled around and trotted south, down the gully between the rolling hills. Bran knew Marcus hadn't yet noticed that he'd put the horse-face brass fixtures on Cu's bridle. He smiled in anticipation of his reaction. Both boys set their faces forward.

They rode south for three hours without stopping. Sometimes they cantered, but more often they trotted quickly. The ground grew flat, with lovely, deep streams and a few rivers in their path. Bran knew the land well and thought it best to avoid both Roman roads and ancient tracks. They rode around many small ditched enclosures and Marcus saw that the land was rich and efficiently farmed. They passed fields of emmer wheat, barley and bread wheat. They also saw fields of flax and of hemp.

'Now you see why your emperors wanted this land,' Bran crowed defiantly. 'We're feeding ourselves *and* selling the surplus to the legions. At least they left our settlements, fields and ancient tracks alone.'

Marcus had grown quite nervous. He had two choices about himself: either he was really seeing spirits or he was growing strange and ill. In any case, he was badly disobeying his parents by travelling, without their knowledge, so far away from Vercovicium.

The boys stopped at a wide, fast-flowing river near Vinovia for lunch. Bran unfolded a large flax cloth to reveal two hard-boiled eggs, a thick slab of rye bread, two cooked breasts of mutton, some delicious-looking hard cheese and ten honey-oat patties. Marcus proudly pulled out of his leather backpack a stuffed hare.

'What's that?' Bran howled. 'What's in it? That's horrible!' He scrunched his face as though he were about to be sick.

'Oh, be quiet! Look, it's just pine kernels, almonds, lots of nuts, dates, whatever.' He turned the hare over and gently pulled apart the underside, showing Bran the stuffing. 'It's good! Try it. I brought some wine cakes too.' He seemed more sure of that.

Bran looked at the wine cakes and still felt ill. Their light yellow colour was strange to him and there were tiny black seeds all through them.

'Oh, the black things are aniseed and the yellow's from cumin and cheese, I think. I don't know! I don't cook, I just sometimes watch them make it and then I eat it. These cakes have wine in them. They're really good. Stop looking that way, Bran. I didn't do that with your food.'

'There's no need with my food. You can tell just by looking at it what it is. Not like this muck!' Bran started to laugh, a little roughly, and jiggled Marcus's pack so all the baked food began to crumble and fall apart.

'Stop that! Stop!' Marcus threw himself on Bran and pinned his arms against the ground. But they were evenly matched and Bran quickly rolled over, simultaneously locking Marcus in a leg hold. Marcus started to fall while Bran slithered out from beneath him.

'Peace, *pax*! I give up. That's enough. Besides, I'm too

hungry to fight. I want to dive into that good Roman muck!
Come on, let's eat.'

Bran's eyes told Marcus that fighting was too dangerous. Marcus nodded, signifying both that he too wanted
to stop and that he understood. They both first drank
from the river before they sat down to their lunch. Neither
spoke as they shared and ate, leaving a good amount for
dinner.

The next two hours' ride took them up a very steep,
wide hill. Marcus wondered if it could be called a mountain.
Curious that there isn't a hillfort up here, he thought. He
was going to ask Bran, but decided not to. It was bad
enough that the Brigantes had lost to the Romans without
his asking about their ancient defences.

Then they rode down the hill on to a very flat plain.
'This can't be where the fortifications are,' Marcus shouted.

'Why not?' Bran shouted back, over the sound of their
horses' hooves.

Marcus felt trapped. He wanted to say, 'Because that
would be stupid! They could be overrun easily,' but stopped
himself. 'I suppose I have a lot to learn about Brigantian
fortifications,' he called, trying to sound cheerful.

Bran shot him a look.

Though the ground was flat, it wasn't all fields. There
were woods everywhere and they passed many small quar-
ries. They had to slow down their horses. Bran grew more
and more cheerful. He was terribly proud of his tribe's seat.
He knew the Brigantes had dominated this huge area for
decades and now he was about to show his Roman friend

117

the centre of their power. He wanted Marcus to be impressed today.

Suddenly they were there. Both boys reined in their horses and Marcus stared, open-mouthed. The ramparts were amazing, just as Bran had said. In front of them was a massive wall, built of earth and stone, extending far to the left and right. Marcus could just see the two sides curving around to start a huge enclosure. The wall, over fifteen feet high, was built of mounded earth, supported and topped by sheer stone. Giant slabs of limestone paved the earth before the rampart wall, giving the impression of a deity's massive walkway. When Bran walked his horse up to the rampart, the difference in size showed Marcus just how extraordinarily high and massive this embankment and wall were.

'Bran, it is all you promised,' Marcus began, his eyes shining.

Bran swelled. 'You haven't seen anything yet. We have masses to see!'

With that, he rode off, turning left. Marcus followed quickly, for he remembered how Bran had disappeared inside his settlement's ditches when they'd first gone to his home. Sure enough, Bran disappeared again, but this time Marcus was right behind him. They found themselves inside a ditched enclosure that itself seemed enclosed by the massive ramparts.

'This is wonderful, Bran,' Marcus whispered.

There was something chilling about the smaller enclosure. It had many collapsed houses in it. They weren't beyond repair and might even have been recently inhabited. But the settlement was eerily quiet and felt deserted. The boys tethered their horses to a sturdy bush and began to explore. Something struck Marcus as odd but he couldn't quite tell what it was. He walked carefully over the fields, towards the main houses. Then he realized: the stone houses, though small, were built in the rectangular Roman style. They weren't circular, like Bran's, and they had Roman roof tiles! Nor did they have the curving path to each door that Bran's settlement houses had. Yet they were clustered as roundhouses.

'Bran, why are these houses in the Roman style? Did the legionaries build them?'

'No, Queen Cartimandua had them built.' His tone rebuked Marcus.

'Well, why are the buildings Roman-style, then?' he asked uneasily. He wondered how he had insulted Bran. He was genuinely curious.

'She liked Roman ways, that's all.' He kicked a pebble down into the ditch and both boys watched silently as it bounced and rolled and landed.

'Oh,' Marcus said.

'Look, Marcus!' Bran whirled on him. 'She was our last tribal leader. She agreed to an alliance with Rome and this linked us to the whole Empire.' He looked at the rectangular houses and waved his arm over the settlement. 'You could find lots of Empire things here, like those houses and their tiled roofs, or Samian ware from Gaul, glassware from Aegyptus . . . Lots.'

But Bran seemed sad as well as proud, Marcus thought.

'I wanted to show you all this. I wanted you to know how powerful we once were. From ancient times, this has been our land, our stone cairns, tombs, tors and circles, from one sea to the other. We've always been great warriors, respected by all the tribes surrounding us. But then this clever queen . . . well . . . she saw the Roman ways were better and thought she could have them without surrendering our independence. She thought –' he again smiled ruefully at Marcus – 'she could manipulate the Roman Empire.'

Marcus didn't know what to answer.

'When she had these houses built, I wonder if she realized.' He stopped.

'Realized what?' Marcus looked steadily at his friend.

'Oh, that she was welcoming the end of our people,' he said bleakly.

Both boys stood in silence.

'Bran, not the end of your people,' Marcus stammered. 'You once told me that your mother accepted and even welcomed the fact that things had changed. Does that help you at all?'

Surprisingly, Bran suddenly smiled. 'I'll tell you what has helped me a little. My sister, who's always hated Romans, keeps asking me about Telemachus,' he said, grinning.

Marcus threw back his head and laughed. 'About Telemachus? Asking about him! *Him?* Impossible. And he's too arrogant to notice girls.'

'Oh, I don't think he knows,' Bran confided. 'Anyway,

120

maybe we'll all become family, one way or another,' he said, smiling again at Marcus. Suddenly he asked, 'Marcus, will you live here forever?'

Both comments caught Marcus completely by surprise. The idea of Telemachus becoming seriously involved with a native girl! Impossible. His father would never allow it. Protective of his brother suddenly, he wondered where he was today and remembered he planned to see the Brocolitia site and Coventina's Well. He replied only to the second comment. 'No, I don't think so. I'll be here as long as . . . as long as my mother wants to stay, I suppose, or until my father gets promoted and sent somewhere else.'

'Does your mother want to go soon?' he pressed.

Marcus frowned and hid his expression. He didn't want Bran to read his face. He knew that his parents had been quarrelling a lot lately. If they kept quarrelling, maybe he and Telemachus and their mother would return to Rome. Three months ago Marcus would have liked that, vastly preferred it. But now? He'd changed since living along this edge of the Empire. Knowing Bran and this countryside, seeing his father even as much as he did, had changed him. He wanted to stay. He drawled in a low-key sort of tone, 'No, I think she wants to stay. She is pregnant, you know.'

Bran grinned.

Marcus shrugged in a friendly, offhand way and that ended the conversation satisfactorily for them both.

He looked again at Cartimandua's house. It wasn't a villa, even a small one. He couldn't see a courtyard or the remains of a formal garden, but the house had two floors, a central front entrance and the remains of a veranda around the ground floor. He shivered, partly from the cold afternoon air and partly from a growing sense of unease. 'Something bad has happened here,' he said under his breath.

'Bad?' Bran repeated, his voice growing weary again. He too looked over the whole settlement and earthworks.

Marcus saw his shoulders stoop. 'What's wrong with you, Bran?' he asked.

Bran scowled at Marcus. For a second Bran saw, in his mind's eye, a vision full of people, his tribe. Here they gathered for their annual festivals, games and rituals, or for war, against Venutius or to aid the legions. He saw men proudly strutting, confident in their strength, skills and spirit. He saw the women, delighted, watching their men. Children grinned, happy in the security and vitality of their tribe. He would be nearly old enough to join the men, a Brigante, a warrior. One man came out of the crowd towards Bran, his arm extended in welcome. His height was imposing, exciting. Around his neck he wore a thick torc of braided gold wires, his torso covered in swirling blue tattoos . . . he was smiling.

'Bran! What's wrong with you? Was there a battle here?' Marcus repeated impatiently.

Bran blinked. Again he saw the dilapidated houses and the tall grass, heard the silence. He shook his head, as though to get water out of his ears. He felt covered, soaked, in humiliation. What had happened to his people, his past?

He looked full into Marcus's bunched-up face. 'Yes,

something bad happened here,' he spat out. 'Not a battle.' He looked off into the hills. 'The final battles were fought up there. Fighting for both sides, many men of our tribe died. No.' He looked again at the fortifications. 'This used to be the gathering ground of the Brigantes. Our gathering ground is lost. Our tribe is lost.' He walked rapidly away from Marcus.

There had been enough talking. Marcus was relieved when Bran called out, 'Come on. Let's get the horses and ride around the outside of the biggest rampart.'

Marcus followed him up towards the horses.

'Bran, you put your horse faces on my horse! Thank you. I love them.' Marcus was surprised and delighted. Only a real friend would do that.

Bran grinned, but there was still a tightness in his face, as though strings had pulled the grin into place.

They cantered off, first finding the entrance and then lurching left to ride around the high ditches. The horses' hooves crashed on the flat limestone slabs lying at the base of the high earth-and-stone rampart. Round they went, always keeping the wall to their left. Sometimes the horses skidded or slipped a bit, but both boys were good riders and quickly regained control. It took a long time to canter all the way around the huge embankment, constantly moving. They laughed with the exhilaration of it.

Marcus was still baffled by the site, with its huge earthworks. They are massive, he thought, but absolutely nothing to an advancing Roman army. I know the earthworks are high, but the ground is flat! If Cartimandua knew the Roman ways, she'd have known this fortification could never work as a defensive stronghold. This couldn't have been their fort. Maybe it was meant to show off the tribe's power, he mused, keeping these thoughts to himself.

By now, the afternoon sun had begun to set and the air was freezing. The boys had hardly noticed as they rode, but now they realized they'd better organize a fire and campsite.

'Marcus!' Bran shouted over the horses. 'Shall we make our fire in Cartimandua's house?'

Marcus turned his head in the settlement's direction. 'Oh, Bran.' He gave his friend a pained look. Somehow, the queen's house didn't seem the best place for a Roman or a Brigante boy to sleep. Yet here they were in the ancient fortification and earthworks, together, safely enclosed, and night was falling. It would be fun to sit by a roaring fire, eating the rest of their food. Maybe, Marcus hoped, all this history would begin to seem ancient too. He nodded to Bran, dismounted and tethered his horse. 'Yes, let's sleep in her house.'

Bran grinned and nodded. And together they entered Cartimandua's headquarters.

THE MARKETPLACE

While the boys had been riding across the countryside towards Cartimandua's fortifications and Telemachus had been searching out Coventina's Well, Claudia and Brigit were preparing for their outing in Coria. Grumio had just made a specific request to Claudia and Brigit for some of his favourite fish sauce, liquamen or garum, imported from Baetica. He put it in everything he ate. He loved the sharp, acrid taste of this sauce made from fish entrails that had been salted and left maturing in a vessel for two months. He said the best variety came from anchovies and he mixed it in with fish, pork, chicken and lamb dishes, egg custards, peas, lentils, onions, and even elderberries and porridge.

'Please, madam, fish sauce, liquamen. Please. Yes. Very good.' He peered anxiously into Claudia's eyes. 'Very good for the stomach! Yes! Very good.'

'Yes, Grumio. We can easily get you more.'

'Thank you, madam.' He kissed her hand. 'Me go too?'

'No, Grumio,' she answered kindly but firmly, just catching Brigit's amused but frantic signals. 'We'll be fine. Besides, the weather has completely turned. You have much to do in the garden to get ready for winter.'

'Madam?'

'The garden, Grumio. Much to do!'

'Oh, yes. Oh, yes, madam. The garden. Yes. Plenty, plenty . . . All right,' he ended cheerfully, and quietly left the kitchen.

Claudia watched his face as the expression settled into its familiar pattern, mirroring, if anyone cared to see, his kind and well-meaning thoughts.

'Thank you, madam,' he called from the Praetorium's hallway.

'Goodbye, Grumio. Thank you,' Claudia called back.

Brigit cast her a long-suffering look.

'Well, I know he's simple, but I am beginning to

understand that he is a very good man,' Claudia mused, answering the look in Brigit's eyes. 'There is a kindness in him that impresses and touches me. From time to time I also catch glimpses of that scout Gaius assures me is in there somewhere. I think I could count on him if ever I or my family were in trouble.'

Brigit started slightly at these words. 'Why would any harm come to you or your family?' she asked.

'Oh, I don't want to think about it. As Gaius keeps reminding me, we are in a war zone.' She stopped wrapping herself with her shawl and leaned against the kitchen wall, smiling. 'Maybe Grumio is a spy. He used to be able to find out any enemy headquarters and report back to Gaius. Funny, isn't it, when he seems so feeble now.'

Brigit was staring at Claudia, riveted by her words. Claudia, however, hadn't noticed as she swirled her shawl around her and, after tossing one long end over a shoulder, secured the two parts of the shawl together with a pretty bronze cloak hook shaped like a sea-horse.

Claudia continued happily: 'Anyway, Samian ware! Pretty glass vases and bowls! A supply officer from Coria told me the merchant there has glass from the Rhineland as well as the Mediterranean. Let us go! We've only been to Coria once since my arrival.'

'If you recall from that visit, there isn't much there. It would be more fun to be going to Eboracum,' she added wistfully, glancing at Claudia.

Claudia caught the look. 'Oh, I know. But that takes *days*. We can at least take a look at what the local farmers are offering and what the traders have. Who knows what we might see, even at this crossroads. The whole Empire lies down those roads! Furthermore, I wish to be accompanied only by you – no ladies' maids, no retinue of servants. Just us – to play!'

She felt extremely cheerful. The boys were doing well. They were on good terms with their father, even if they saw him only briefly at dinner. They were studying, exercising and taking an interest in their surroundings. And, after a period of quarrelling, she and Gaius were getting along well. Best of all, the pregnancy was healthy. She had passed the first trimester and felt wonderful. She was not showing yet, but anyone familiar with pregnancy would know.

With the autumn the weather had turned cold, but was not yet freezing. The two ladies wore layers of soft woollen shawls, the softest tied at the waist and below the breasts. Over their gowns they'd thrown *pallae*, lovely soft woollen mantles. Though both were similarly dressed, Brigit's ensemble declared her loyalty to the Brigante love of colour, unlike Claudia's sedate Roman shades. As they walked down the Praetorium's corridor, Claudia looked at Brigit with surprise.

'What is on your face?' she teased.

Brigit blushed. 'Look!' She pulled out of her woven tapestry bag a little alabaster pot that was corked. She opened it and dipped in a fine brush she'd also taken from her bag. Very carefully she applied the lip tint to Claudia's lips. 'Stop smiling,' she said, laughing herself. She replaced the pot and brush in her bag, then extricated two lovely, delicate glass phials. Upending one, she released into her palm a few grains of ochre, dark red in colour. Placing that phial on the corridor floor, she quickly upended the other one and out came a drop of lanolin, from unwashed sheep's wool. Mixing them together quickly with her finger, she expertly dabbed Claudia's cheeks with the red liquid, rubbing in a circular, upward fashion.

'What are you doing to me?' Claudia shrieked.

The two of them began giggling, like young girls.

'Quiet. One more thing,' Brigit sternly reprimanded her. With great care and, Claudia noticed, pride, Brigit now pulled out of her bag a delicate wooden box, smaller than the palm of her hand. It had been finely crafted in tiny pieces of wood marquetry of several different types and contrasting colours. Her fingers closed around it gently and sought out the hidden spring latch. Claudia watched breathlessly. As the top lifted, Claudia saw what seemed magic dust – beautiful silver bits that would fly away if breathed upon.

'Oh,' Claudia whispered. 'Where did you find antimony? I've not seen any since Rome!'

Not answering, Brigit dipped her little finger into the silver dust and silently, ever so carefully, ran it along Claudia's eyebrows, leaving sparkles among the thick, brown hairs. Then both women again burst out laughing and ran back up the corridor to Claudia's bedroom. Claudia got there first and went straight to the table where she kept her highly polished, decorated hand-mirror. Looking at herself, she blushed.

'Brigit! I can't go out like this! I am carrying a child! And the wife of the Prefect! I look like some painted doll from an ancient tomb in Aegyptus!'

At that, Brigit collapsed into giggles, setting Claudia off again.

As Claudia rocked with laughter, her eyes tightly shut, Brigit's laughter trailed off. She glanced at Claudia's hand-mirror and remembered again the bronze hand-mirror she had inherited from her mother, and she from her mother, and she from hers. She remembered its basket-weave decoration and the hidden face. The metalwork on her mirror was superior to Claudia's, yet as always she felt inferior, subsidiary. In her own land. Neither Roman nor properly Brigante. Anger and shame rose up in her. She *liked* Claudia but was beginning to feel that she could no longer continue living in two worlds. The land was her people's and she must work to free it, for all Claudia's kindness.

'You look fine. You look the ideal Prefect's wife,' she said steadily. She wanted to fall back into their happy mood, but could not. 'Let us go quickly or we'll never get away from here.'

Claudia was surprised by her tone but didn't resist. She rather enjoyed being passive these days. It's the pregnancy, she thought cheerfully. Funny day, she said to herself, as they padded down the corridor, soft leather shoes swishing, and out of the Praetorium, into the waiting cart.

The journey gave Brigit time to compose herself. The two women drew up their shopping lists, had a nap, then began to look out and enjoy the countryside. Their cart, escorted by two cavalry, had gone out through the causeway and joined the cart road heading east. Soon they came to the main north–south road built by the legions and turned south, reaching Coria after a bumpy ride. The fort at Coria had been a military outpost since the legions had taken over the Brigantian lands. Originally it had been a timber fort and now, rebuilt in stone, it served as an important supply centre for the Wall, storing a tremendous amount of grain. The town had become a lively commercial centre.

'Oh, look,' Claudia said, nudging Brigit as their cart rumbled down the stone street through the village. 'See, potters and leather workers. And there's the fish shop, the bakery and the wine shop. I'd forgotten how many shops were here. How rude of you – a Brigante – to have called Coria a crossroads!' Claudia tossed a smile at Brigit while busily surveying the scene. 'I want to go first to that tavern for some food. Do you agree?'

Wincing inwardly at Claudia's little jibe, Brigit still replied cheerfully, 'I do. Some bread and olives, nettle soup and then a honey sweet would be perfect. Where did we go last time? It was just midsummer then.'

They both gazed absent-mindedly from the window until their cart stopped outside the tavern. They descended demurely, sweeping their layered dresses and *pallae* gracefully before and behind them as they stepped up into the tavern and chose a secluded area. Sturdy wooden tables with wooden stools were placed about the comfortable room. The tavern was famous for its wide variety of imported liquamen, so Claudia ordered two large amphorae for Grumio.

After they had eaten, they strolled down the main street. Each shop had an open front. Inside were goods neatly piled and shelved. Claudia knew, from Rome, that usually the shopkeeper and his or her family lived above the shop. The first shop that caught their attention was a fish-monger's, presided over by an astonishing woman. She was beautiful, very tall and generously built, with flaxen blonde hair and piercing blue eyes. In a voice so loud it could carry to the sea, she announced her wares, which were abundantly displayed around her. She spoke her Latin with a strong Germanic accent and her blue eyes flashed out mischievously at all her customers. At her side, shadow-ing her every step, was a large, comfortable-looking dog, who clearly worshipped her. He kept close to her all the time they were watching, his nose touching his mistress's knee. The ladies could tell she was a favourite with the customers and smiled to see her laugh and joke with each one in turn.

'She is a real Nehalennia, isn't she?' Brigit whispered to Claudia.

'Who is Nehalennia?' Claudia whispered back, smiling at the scene.

'She's a goddess worshipped along both coasts of the North Sea. I came to know about her when I lived briefly on the east coast. Seafarers and travellers pray to her for safe conduct, but, as you can see, she is loved by everyone. And look at her dog! Nehalennia is famous for her adoring dog, always at her side.' The ladies gave their Nehalennia a parting smile and walked on, soon coming to the potter's shop.

Just before they entered, though, Brigit caught sight, across the street, of Modron, her relative, Bran's mother. Confusion rose up in her heart. Should she introduce Modron to Claudia or slip immediately into the potter's shop and avoid her? Somehow, she felt, her own fate was involved in the encounter.

Her instinct told her to act, to trust the kindness and empathy in each woman. Why shouldn't they meet? She shook herself and, taking Claudia's arm, whispered into her ear, 'Do you see that ginger-haired Brigante buying dyes, over in the cloth merchant's shop?'

Claudia took a moment, then saw the shop and the woman.

'Oh, yes. My, she is attractive, isn't she?' Claudia rejoined agreeably.

'Claudia, her name is Modron and she is Bran's mother and my relative. She weaves the most beautiful cloth. Would you like to meet her? Her Latin is excellent and we can find out how the boys are.'

Claudia was momentarily disorientated. She had immediately remembered that this woman's husband had been killed fighting alongside the legions against the local Britons. Still, she felt uncomfortable. 'Fraternizing with the natives, especially when there are hostilities, is inadvisable,' Gaius had often warned. Modron was studying the garishly coloured bolts of cloth. 'I am lonely for women friends,' Claudia imagined herself telling Gaius, 'and this woman and

I have something in common: we both raised our children alone, due to war. How dangerous can this "native" be to me?'

'Yes, please, do introduce me,' she answered as they crossed the street, first carefully stepping over the high but covered drain, and then avoiding mud and animal excrement in the street.

Brigit managed the introductions gracefully and soon the three women were chatting easily. Fascinated, Claudia looked closely at Modron's dress. It was of woven wool, dyed red (with madder, she guessed) and decorated with purple tapestry-woven bands. She's very good at weaving – and look at those corded borders! Maybe she could weave for me, she thought.

Both Claudia and Brigit could see rapid calculations pass over Modron's face as she adjusted her expression to meet the Prefect's wife. By any political consideration, they should have been shy with each other, but, as Brigit had anticipated, the two women felt an instant rapport. Brigit watched Modron closely, to see how a widowed Brigante held herself with the commander's wife, but Modron kept any reaction well hidden.

The three women got along so well that soon a plan was made for them all to return to Modron's settlement, to show Claudia something of the Brigantian ways. Claudia pushed from her mind the certainty that Gaius would disapprove.

She considered praying to Vesta, but the Roman goddess seemed irrelevant somehow. She thought about praying to the Three Mothers. Brigit had told her the Brigante women prayed to them for a good pregnancy and childbirth. How maddening to have to pray to Vesta in Rome but to the Three Mothers in northern Britannia! These goddesses must be related or connected or know about each other. It's all too ridiculous otherwise, she thought crossly. Suddenly she made up her mind to go to Modron's home.

She did not notice Brigit and Modron watching her, surprised at her decision to come to the settlement. They knew it was unusual and would not be approved of. This was a special Roman wife before them, their expressions seemed to conclude.

'I do need to ask how rough or bumpy the ride there is, though,' Claudia said to Modron. A smile beamed out from Claudia's face as she confided, 'I am pregnant after all!'

Modron smiled back, reflecting this beautiful Roman lady's happiness.

'Do not worry. We travel back along the same legions' road and the cart road that you came on,' she assured Claudia. 'Quite near the causeway for Vercovicium, we will need to leave your cart and walk a short distance. It is up- and downhill, but I think you will be fine. After all, I did it during my pregnancies with Rhiannon and Bran, and look at them now!' She grinned with maternal pride. 'Your escorts can easily lend an arm if you grow weary.'

Claudia basked in Modron's welcome. As all three women entered her cart, she asked Modron how and where the boys were.

'Oh, I imagine they're fine!' Modron answered, laughing, though also a little surprised that Claudia didn't know more of what her son was up to. 'They promised to camp somewhere near our settlement, but I'm fairly sure they have a plot afoot. Bran dearly wants to take Marcus down south to the ancient Brigantian gathering place. He knows I wouldn't be likely to give permission, as it is really quite a distance – about thirty miles – and over a varied terrain of streams, rivers and one very large hill. But Bran knows the countryside well and is dying to show off Queen Cartimandua's fortifications to his Roman friend!' She saw Claudia's face suffuse with a deep blush of surprise and then alarm. 'Oh, don't worry, please! They won't come to any harm. Any political unrest is far north-east of there, beyond the Wall. No one would bother about two twelve-year-old boys!'

Claudia looked down to cover her confusion. Brigit understood but also kept quiet. They both knew, despite Modron's confidence, that even in Brigantian territory a Prefect's son was never completely safe. Raiding parties from the tribes north and west of the Brigantes might well slip south of the Wall to attack.

Modron was aware of the sudden silence. Uncertain of what to say to calm Claudia, she filled the gap by chatting. 'You know, Coria is the main trading centre for the Brigantes now, from north and south of the Wall. This is the place where we tend to meet ... now that the Wall separates us.' She was in confusion and wished she'd never begun this topic.

Claudia looked up, her fears deepening. 'Brigantes

from the north come south through the Wall to Coria? This is where the tribal families gather?' She was thinking of evenings over the past few weeks when Gaius had patiently explained to Telemachus where the risks Vercovicium faced came from. She usually sat near them, sewing. 'The point is, we must juggle our different jobs. We protect here –' and Gaius would sweep his hand over the map laid out before them, indicating all the lands south of the Wall – 'we hold our outpost forts all up here –' quickly pointing to the nine or so forts north of the Wall, while boring his eyes into Telemachus's – 'and simultaneously we prepare for our northern advance!' Just for a second, Claudia felt a flicker of a smile as she remembered their shared excitement. Then she was awash with worry.

Modron continued: 'Farmers, miners, merchants, artisans – we all gather here, most often on market days. I meet people I haven't seen for whole seasons!' She glanced at Claudia's worried face and, in distress, immediately stopped speaking. 'Please tell me! What is upsetting you?'

Claudia covered her mouth with her hand and blushed. She was completely confused and didn't want to make a fool of herself. Her fears were like bees, swarming around her. Were they real or just the agitations of a pregnant woman? Modron thought the boys were safe. She knew the area and the people. Surely she would never let any harm come to her own son or to a boy entrusted to her safe-keeping. In such ways, Claudia's mind strove to find calm, to quiet her fears and guilt.

'I'm fine.' She nodded and smiled, casting quick looks at

each woman. 'I think I am easily moved these days.' Then she laughed, encircling the under part of her tummy with one arm. Her belly was hardly bulging yet, but her arm remembered the gesture from her previous pregnancies. 'We've only been here a few months and I am still unfamiliar with much of the land. You say these earthworks are far south of the Wall?' she asked Modron.

'Yes,' Modron assured her. 'It's halfway to Eboracum! I imagine they'll ride on or near the main north–south road. There must be four or five forts between here and there on that road. They'll come to no harm, I'm sure.' She looked quickly but deeply into Claudia's eyes to read her heart. Why was this Roman lady so afraid? Was there some trouble brewing?

To cover her confusion, she lifted her head to the two ladies and said, 'Shall we make our way to my settlement? I would be honoured to show you where and how we live. Please,' she finished, reassuring both herself and Claudia with her kindness.

Well, Claudia thought, there was nothing she could do about Marcus – not until he returned. But she might see this settlement and learn more about the Brigantes closest to Vercovicium.

Brigit watched the other women in silence. She envied them their positions in their worlds. Modron was born, raised and married in this part of Brigantium. She had been respected before her widowhood for her fine weaving and now she was even more respected for having raised her children, looked after her land and home, and continued to sell her wool cloth so successfully. Claudia, the elegant wife of the Prefect, well established in Rome, the mother of two sons, had high status wherever she went in the Empire. Brigit thought, I have no such position, no place in either's world. But her greatest envy was of their motherhood. Four children between them, five soon, and I have none, she thought. She wanted to belong. She wanted someone to belong to her. I mustn't show this anger, she told herself. Rearrange your face. They are becoming friends. Look calm and pleased for them. I must not alienate these women, whatever my connection with their cultures.

INSIDE THE ROUNDHOUSE

The cart made its way back up the north–south road and west along the cart road. Instead of turning north to Vercovicium and the Wall, it continued a bit further along the cart road and then veered south, on to a farm track made by the feet of oxen, cattle and horses, and the wheels of carts. Soon they had to stop, as the slope became too steep.

The ride had given Claudia time to think. She reasoned that Gaius would know about Coria. After all, the crossroads had been strategically important since Agricola took the north. And Modron's settlement, so close to Vercovicium, couldn't be hostile. As for the ancient Brigantian gathering place, Marcus had behaved foolishly and irresponsibly by going there, and would be punished tomorrow night, but Modron said it was safe. These thoughts settled her. She admitted she was curious about Modron and her home. Brigit kept her Brigantian bonds very quiet at Vercovicium. Now Claudia would learn something of her other life. She thought with interest, tinged with suspicion, that it was odd she'd not yet been to the farm where Brigit lived. That she was allowing herself an adventure similar to Marcus's did not occur to her.

Climbing the final hill on foot was hard for Claudia, but she made it, weaving her way with the others through the two earthwork defences, and arrived at the top, in the walled settlement. All three women felt there was no need to have the military guards, who would only be conspicuous and alarming in this peaceful setting. Modron took her two visitors immediately into her hut and raked the fire until it crackled. Claudia was as amazed as Marcus had been at the huge size of the hut. She too jumped at the sound and sight of large beasts rustling behind the woven-birch wall, but felt, even more than Marcus had, the enveloping warmth of the dark, circular structure. She sat happily with Brigit by the fire on a shaped log, while Modron bustled about the enclosure. Brigit settled in comfortably, obviously familiar with the roundhouse.

The first thing Modron did was to unloop a long and magnificent iron-link chain from the side of the room, bringing its end to hang close over the fire. Two elegant dog-shaped fire irons held the burning logs in place. Claudia followed the chain with her eyes and saw it was suspended from a rectangle of cross-rafters right at the peak of the ceiling.

'By Nantosuelta,' Modron exclaimed in irritation, 'I'm out of milk. I have some burstin and thought we might like that with milk, but there is none.' Claudia looked so blankly at her it made Modron laugh. 'Burstin, you must know it. Have you never had it? It's an ancient dish, older than the hills beneath us, made with barley. I'll show you as soon as I borrow some milk from my neighbour.'

Brigit reassured her, saying, 'Don't worry, Modron. Here, I'll go with you. Let me first show off to Claudia what you do with the barley.'

Modron was flattered, but she was wary too. She knew such a simple hot cereal might seem 'barbaric' to a sophisticated Roman lady. There again, she knew it tasted good and was the perfect food to eat when tired, cold, hungry and, she smiled, pregnant. She looked carefully at Claudia. No, she isn't going to scorn us when she gets back to the fort. In fact, Modron thought Claudia seemed truly at ease and happy, which made her wonder about her daily life at Vercovicium. Modron also wondered at Brigit's bustling. She certainly doesn't help like this when she's visiting alone, she noted. Quite the grand Roman lady.

Brigit picked up a lovely bowl that was resting near the fire. It was squat, with an elegant design of circles and swirls deftly scratched into the clay surface. Claudia must see how intricate this recipe is, she thought happily, how rich our culture is. But first she reached into the pot, showing Claudia a palmful of golden, long-eared grains. 'To begin with she gleans this barley grain – we call it six-row – from the barley stalk, and then she dries the grain by the fire in

140

this bowl. Next, she grinds the dried grain on a quern, making a rich brown meal called burstin. She'll add warmed milk to the meal and we'll have a wonderful, filling porridge.'

Claudia watched Brigit's face while she recited the recipe and acted out the steps. There was something heart-breaking in it, but she wasn't sure why. I don't think she has ever done this herself, she thought with surprise. She's trying to impress me. Or is she afraid I'll mock all this when I get back to Gaius? Claudia gazed, puzzled, at Brigit. They were good companions, but Claudia realized how little she knew of her. Brigit was a mystery.

Claudia said aloud, 'Nothing would be more welcome now on this chilly afternoon than burstin. Yes, please.' She smiled in Modron's direction, purposely avoiding Brigit's eyes. She somehow felt unsure of her friend, embarrassed. 'It's extremely soothing to sit here. I don't think I've been as relaxed as this since leaving Rome.' She sighed, obviously tired, but soothed by the warmth of the fire.

Modron nodded, for she had seen Claudia's growing ease for herself. Claudia smiled encouragingly at the other two women, who then left, ducking beneath the heavy woven cloth hanging over the doorway.

The invisible animals shifted behind the birch screen and a large glowing stick from the fire broke apart and fell into the flames. The hut held the air, still, warm, safe. Claudia lay back against some sacks of wheat and day-dreamed, remembering stories of the local gods told to her by Brigit and Grumio. When she fell pregnant, Brigit told her about the Three Mothers and about her own namesake goddess, Brigantia, who would protect her during her pregnancy and help her when the birthing time came. Claudia remembered the small stone relief Brigit had given her of the Mothers, shown seated, holding in their laps nursing infants. Sometimes they held baskets of fruit, loaves of bread or fish, Brigit told her. Brigit carefully explained how these symbols reminded the Mothers' worshippers of fertility. Anyone who's had children to feed every day knows about such symbols of fertility, Claudia thought. Grumio had bought Claudia a clay statuette of Dea Nutrix, seated in a high-backed wicker chair, nursing her infant. He told her she should keep this statuette safe, as it would protect her. Claudia smiled in the semi-darkness, happy in the safety and thoughtfulness of her two friends and their new gods.

She felt a warmth creep over her, almost holding her. The feeling was so real she started to worry, but then she surrendered to the spell. The fire crackled, the large beasts behind her lazily stomped their hooves, and the sense of being embraced – securely, gently – continued. She began to doze, thinking of the Celtic god Sucellus and his consort Nantosuelta. Marcus had told her about these gods. She smiled to remember: she had been told by Marcus, Marcus had been told by Bran, Bran had been told by Rhiannon and Rhiannon had been told by her father, long ago. I wonder who told her father? she thought, gazing into the fire. Marcus said the Celtic hammer god and his wife reminded their worshippers of the importance of home life.

I love being a mother, she thought, smiling a little sadly, but I am lonely; beneath it all, I am. I would like to play a larger part in Gaius's thoughts and feelings. I need something more and I have more to give. I want to be like Modron, she suddenly realized. Making ancient recipes, living in the centre of a roundhouse. Oh, I don't know what I'm saying! She shook her head. Could it be that Marcus and his mother wish to become Brigantes? No, no, it isn't that, it's something about the way Modron is, about her presence. She is ... and with that unfinished thought, Claudia fell asleep.

She dreamed of a man's voice, deep and quiet. It whispered, 'Your baby, your boy, has been conceived on Brigantian land. He has drunk, through you, Brigantian water and been warmed by the Brigantian sun. His father is Roman, but he is ours. We watch over him. Epona asks her horses at Vercovicium to pass the word back to us when you ride out, when you stay in. Coventina and Sulis provide the water that flows into your cistern to make your bath, asking it to spy upon you and flow back to tell us. The *genii cucullati* – our woodland gnomes – are always around you, protecting you, protecting your baby, who is ours.'

Claudia started. Still half asleep, she wanted to move but couldn't. She was somehow being held, restrained. She felt a man's arms around her and, when she turned her head to see him, she felt the cold metal of a necklace against her cheek. She could see no one, but now her cheek was brushed by a soft moustache. A feeling of calm spread through her and she no longer wanted to resist. She swooned into a deeper sleep, feeling herself falling through space, down under the ground and back into time. The man's words swirled in her head: 'Your baby has been conceived on Brigantian land. He has drunk, through you, Brigantian water and been warmed by the Brigantian sun. The *genii cucullati* are always around you, protecting you, protecting your baby, who is ours.' Ours, she repeated, ours. Then she woke.

'The baby is mine. It is mine and Gaius's. He's a Roman baby,' she shouted into the centre of the roundhouse, into the fire. The cattle shifted uneasily behind her, making her start too in surprise. What is happening? she thought. What a terrifying dream. Who is watching me, speaking to my horses?

She looked around and saw nobody. She settled back again on to the wheat sacks behind her. It is true my baby was conceived here and will drink Brigantian water and be warmed by the Brigantian sun, she thought, but he is Roman. She sighed. What will be his future? Her future? What future will the Empire offer my children? It will be a different Empire from the one I grew up with. I was born soon after Trajan became Emperor and all the world seemed destined to become Roman. Has the Empire discovered its limits? Will its growth be different somehow, a weaving together of conquered and conquerors? She slowly rubbed her belly. What will be the way forward for my children, for my Romano-Brigante baby? she wondered, and smiled.

At that moment, Brigit and Modron returned. Modron hooked the cauldron on to the suspended chain and poured milk from a pitcher. Once it had warmed, she ladled it into three grooved bowls, each with a little pottery spoon, and instructed her guests to mix the burstin and milk. Claudia accepted her bowl and spoon quietly, hardly moving. The two relatives exchanged sympathetic glances, tacitly acknowledging that the day had been too strenuous for their silent, pregnant friend.

THE STRATEGY

Quintus Valerius leaned back, stretched his legs and crushed another sweet chestnut.

'You see, Prefect, I have it all figured out.'

'You do?' Gaius answered, with a wry smile.

Quintus passed the brass bowl over to him.

'Yes. The Wall's defensive system is nearing completion. Two, three more years and we will have forts, milecastles and turrets all across the land and down the west coast. I mean, even Brocolitia is nearly finished. Yes?' He reached for another chestnut, accidentally tipping the hammered brass bowl. Before Gaius could answer, Quintus continued: 'It is growing cold, Gaius! Another winter on the Wall for us.' He smiled companionably.

'Another winter, yes. But what exactly have you figured out? That the Wall's defences are almost finished? Did you notice that all by yourself?' Gaius took a chestnut and passed the bowl back to Quintus.

'Here's what I've been thinking,' Quintus said. 'I've been stationed at this fort for nearly two years. Over the past ten, you have watched the Wall and the earthwork defences go up and seen the countryside divided. Our fort is an important one, near Coria and the main north–south road. To prevent attack, say by a band of men from the northern tribes, what is our strategy?'

'First, we always have our spies and scouts,' Gaius replied.

'Right,' said Quintus.

'Then, at regular intervals throughout the day, each fort sends out local patrols, both foot and cavalry. These are especially important coming from and reporting back to the frontier forts, Banna and Blatobulgium – the local patrols are our warning eyes, to spot trouble from the north.'

'Yes,' Quintus agreed.

'Then we have the Wall forts, milecastles and turrets,' said Gaius.

Quintus nodded.

'The *alae* at Luguvalium and Cilurnium are available to us?' Gaius asked, smiling, seeing the point his centurion was building to.

'Yes.' Quintus smiled back.

'And finally the legions marching up from Eboracum and over and up from Deva?'

'Yes.' Quintus nodded.

'We know how many men are meant to be assigned to each unit, but how many could we actually count on in an emergency?' Gaius asked him.

'All right,' replied the centurion. 'Let me add it up. Cavalry on the Wall, two thousand; forward of the Wall, one thousand; close behind the Wall in the road forts, another one thousand – giving us four thousand cavalry. As for the infantry, three and a half thousand on the Wall, two and a half thousand forward and two thousand in the road forts – a total of eight thousand. All in all, twelve thousand soldiers available within two or three days of a major alarm. Of course, add to that the two legions from Eboracum and Deva with their four thousand men each – they could get to us within a couple of weeks. And how many enemy are there, if you combine them – as if they'd ever join in organized combat?' Quintus was enjoying his game and was now ready to pounce.

Gaius waved his hand with impatient disregard.

'Right,' agreed Quintus. 'Not enough to worry us, and we know they'd never join up in an organized army. Leave aside the Caledonian tribes for a moment. They are far enough north not to concern us right now. We are not going to face a sustained, integrated attack. We are going to face raids – thieving, stealing cattle, women, slaves – raids to please them and humiliate us. Some of our men will be killed. Our job is to minimize deaths, and secure and resecure our control. We have to be alert and keep our spy system extended, send out the patrols. But we'll keep our eye on Caledonia the whole time too, looking to the future. We are an offensive army and there is nothing – no serious force – threatening us. Our time of expansion will come.' Quintus stopped and looked at his commander.

Gaius fixed Quintus with a hard stare. Then, though he remained still, his gaze turned inward and he began to think. It was true that he'd come to think of Vercovicium and the other forts along the Wall as 'holding the line', even though they all constantly sent out patrols and kept in close touch with Banna, Blatobulgium and other frontier forts. His had become a siege mentality. Yet the whole system of the Wall and the forts was still new. Never before in the Empire's history had the Emperor and his legions set out to encircle the Roman world with walls, deserts, mountains and rivers. To bring expansion to an end. He smiled at his centurion.

'You have a point. If the Emperor has sent us here to keep us occupied and away from Rome, we shall give him an impressive show of control, but then, of course, we shall make our move.'

Quintus nodded. He rose and absent-mindedly spun the brass bowl round like a top. 'Until tomorrow,' he said, and strode out of the office and the Principia.

The bowl rattled in its spin while Gaius, smiling, continued to sit and gaze inwardly. It's true, he thought. No serious threats and the future lies before us.

ROAST GOOSE

Gaius reclined on the central couch and held out his glass for honeyed wine. The slave filled his glass, and then the glasses of Claudia and Telemachus. Marcus had returned just before dinner, to be greeted by a stony-faced father and tremulous mother. He had been sent directly to his room for the night, no dinner. They agreed to discuss his 'outing', as Gaius put it, in the morning. Now that Marcus was, in fact, safely home and in bed, his parents felt mightily

148

relieved. Although Claudia was still subdued from her dis-
quieting dream at Modron's, Gaius was jovial, happy his
son was safe and confident after his meeting with Quintus.

Now he looked at his wife and elder son with great good
humour. He reviewed the recent good turns in his family's
fortunes: Claudia had become pregnant; Telemachus had
progressed in his studies, in combat practice and in scouting
with Grumio; and Marcus – here his face darkened – what
had Marcus been up to these four months? Gaius knew
he'd been with Titus Helius daily, but not as intensively as
Telemachus. He would have to look into Marcus's routine
more closely. He was a dreamy boy, thoughtful. Gaius had
seen that the day they arrived. Hard to know what career
might be best for him. Have to think about that. He glanced
again at Claudia and noted that she seemed withdrawn. No
doubt the pregnancy, he thought, with satisfaction. 'If they
become pregnant, they will be cured.' He smiled to himself.
Yes, now we rarely quarrel and she's been well occupied by
the garden, Brigit and the boys. Good.

'Telemachus, what did you do today?' Gaius asked in an
unusually exuberant tone.

Telemachus raised his eyebrows while still looking
down at the table laden with dishes of lettuce and leeks and
of green and black olives. He pressed his lips together and
turned his head to his father, saying, 'Oh, not much, Father.
I decided to see Coventina's Well over near Brocolitia.'

'Ah! How is the construction of Brocolitia coming
along?' he replied, drinking some wine. 'What did you make
of the well? Clever how the engineers formed it, boxing

the stream in lead pipes.' He smiled, tossing back the last of his drink.

Again Telemachus paused before answering. He had a choice of two questions, but seemed to be looking for his words. Gaius observed him closely.

'Brocolitia seems to be coming along fine. There was a lot of activity there. I saw the temple to Mithras.' He quickly looked up at his father, then paused again. 'I found the well site a little disappointing. It was interesting that the source of the stream was so high up the slope and near the cliff edge. But I . . .' He faltered. 'I did feel a bit let down and so walked down the slope, across the cart road, and found the . . . um . . . river over that southern ridge and another pool dedicated to Coventina.' He finished with an unsuccessful attempt at a careless air.

Gaius's face had grown completely still. He reached out to the little dishes of food and, by deftly scrabbling with his wide hand, collected some olives. The slave poured more wine. Claudia was looking carefully at Telemachus now. Something in his embarrassment alerted her also to untold parts of his account. She sipped her wine but didn't eat.

'The cult of Mithras is an ancient one involving severe tests and training,' Gaius said, slowly nodding to his son to show he understood the boy's inadmissible interest in this secret sect. 'But what of this pool? Who told you it was dedicated to Coventina?'

His guess was a shrewd one, bringing out a burning blush in Telemachus. After all, the auxiliaries had told Telemachus about Coventina's Well, but no one had described the natural pool by the stream. Rhiannon had told him that this was her special pool. Both Gaius and Claudia were surprised, but Gaius was the quicker to recover. In a voice made more frightening by its quiet, he asked, 'Telemachus, who have you been seeing?'

'I haven't "been seeing" anyone!' he blurted. 'I happened to run into the same Brigante girl I ran into months ago, when we first arrived. That day we actually collided, but this time she came upon me at the pool and told me about Coventina. She's Bran's sister, Father,' he said, looking for the first time into Gaius's face.

Somehow his eyes were alerting his father to trouble. Gaius understood that Telemachus was urging him to see this second encounter as acceptable. Claudia's worried eyes asked the same question: why wouldn't this encounter be acceptable?

Gaius held Telemachus's look, his expression darkening. 'I don't want you *socializing* with the Brigantes. Is that clear?' Claudia could see his expression harden. The sinews on his neck were beginning to swell; his head was absolutely still.

Telemachus's face reddened. 'Why?'

'Because I said so.'

Telemachus had the look of a bull about to charge. 'Are you not being a hypocrite?'

Total surprise registered on his parents' faces.

'You're a native! You're a Batavian native, from a tribe, just like Bran and his sister. Your greatest hero was a native, from a *tribe*: Gnaeus Julius Agricola, who "subdued

Britannia", was from Forum Julii. And Hadrian Augustus himself is a native, from Baetica! None of these men are Romans, from Rome.'

The boy's tone, clearly challenging, drew all his father's rage. Gaius's eyes promised more violence than Telemachus could have anticipated. 'Don't you ever again speak to me like that,' he roared into his son's face.

Claudia felt a violent tightening of her stomach and feared for the baby. Just then slaves entered to clear away the *gustatio*, the first course, as other slaves set the table with plates of fresh, boiled broccoli and roast goose. The three Romans immediately assumed inscrutable expressions, father and son looking into the middle distance. The scent of the food began to distract them, much to Claudia's relief. There was silence as they began slowly to eat and drink.

By tacit agreement, it was Gaius who spoke first, in a detached, formal tone. He looked directly into Telemachus's eyes. 'It is true I was born in Batavia, of the equestrian class. It is also true that I rose, especially through active service in Dacia, to be Prefect of this distinguished *milliaria peditata* cohort at Vercovicium.'

Silence.

'I am a native. I am a citizen. I have been honoured by two emperors. This is how we spread the benefits of the Empire, how our conquered peoples become swayed by *romanitas*, the civilized ways of Rome. With the help of all the gods, I might one day become a prefect of an *ala milliaria*, appointed personally by the Emperor.' Gaius seemed almost to hammer this speech into Telemachus, his impertinent son. 'My career has been different from that of my brother in Rome, who, as a quaestor, has been able to earn further advancement while at the centre of government and not in the dangerous, tribal provinces of Dacia or northern Britannia, for instance. It is my hope he will help you, through our mutual sense of family. Then you too –' he shot anger straight into Telemachus's eyes – 'may, as members of the equestrian class, rise to the senatorial class. Are we hypocrites for wanting to better ourselves, Telemachus?'

Telemachus now looked straight ahead, not at his father. His neck was red and his jaw muscles tight.

'To succeed, I must control this area of northern Britannia. This control begins in my own Praetorium. We are controlling the Brigantes, Telemachus, not befriending them.' His voice was now cold and hard. 'Nor, I might add –' and now he turned his gaze to Claudia – 'are we here to roam the countryside, as Marcus has been doing.'

Claudia was dizzy with fear, first for Telemachus, then for herself and now for Marcus.

'Telemachus, you may be excused,' she said quietly, firmly, as though in full support of her husband, though both men knew she was helping her son escape.

Telemachus slid back off the chaise, bowed to his parents, his face a mask, and left the room. He wanted to leave, to think. Why had he said those things to his father? What had stirred him up this way?

Gaius and Claudia began to eat again in silence. The slaves returned to pour the wine and then to bring out the *mensa secunda*, grapes and cheese seasoned in wine.

'The boys are not to spend time with the Brigantes, Claudia,' Gaius said quietly, not inviting discussion.

But she knew Marcus thought only about being with Bran, and now some awful intimacy had grown up with Telemachus. Poor boy, she thought. Has he fallen in love – and with a local? She glanced at Gaius, wondering if he saw the irony of his being a native and having married a Roman lady, while his son, a Roman, seemed to be having a flirtation with a native girl. No, he didn't see it.

'Both boys are loyal Romans. We have every reason to be proud of them.' Having spoken, she sipped her wine.

'This settlement of Bran and his family may be Brigit's native home, but our sons are not to go there. Even if this order is awkward for you to implement, I command it.'

Again silence. Her mind slipped into reverie. What was that dream in Modron's roundhouse? she wondered. Had she been visited by a local spirit? She well remembered the wonderful embrace she'd felt during the dream. Never had she felt so wanted and safe. She looked over at Gaius.

She sought a way to soften Gaius's dictum, for the boys' sakes – but also for her own. She wanted to be able to visit the roundhouse, to see Modron, to let Marcus see Bran – ah! – even, she now realized, to let Telemachus see Rhiannon. Guilt flooded her mind. Was she going to help some liaison between her son and a native girl, against Gaius's orders? No. Telemachus would have to keep away. She dropped her eyes. Further defiance would only enrage Gaius. To come to this edge of Empire had been Claudia's wish and now she must make it work.

'I have begun to make clothes and wraps for the baby.' She smiled slowly. 'Brigit has shown me some wonderful new weaves, done most expertly on the loom of her relative, Modron, Bran's mother. At least may I, from time to time, visit Modron to order her cloth for the baby?' She held her breath, but made no outward sign that this was anything other than a simple request. As she sat still her body seemed to be conjuring up the memory of her dream. She pushed it from her mind, but eerily felt the arms about her, circling her gently.

Gaius's colour had returned. 'This afternoon I had an interview with Quintus that put me in an excellent mood. That was how I came to dinner,' he said, glancing sideways at his wife.

'Telemachus has grown and is older now. Sixteen-year-old boys are difficult from time to time,' she replied, gently smiling at him, while waiting to hear the decision that would so affect her and her boys. Her mind raced. Who will Marcus play with? What can he do? And what has happened to Telemachus? Aloud, she said, 'I must say, before you answer, Gaius, that I would feel uncomfortable travelling to the settlement with only Brigit and the escort, and would like to take Marcus at least. These would be rare visits, but I would feel better and appreciate your kindness.' Suddenly she winced, as if in pain, crossing her belly with her arm.

'What is it? Is the baby all right?' Gaius called out.

'Oh,' she relaxed. 'That's better. I felt some tightening, but everything feels fine now.'

Gaius rose and walked to her, gently placing his hand on

her belly protectively, as the master of this woman and of the house.

The ruse worked, as she'd hoped, for while his face had been darkening to forbid them, he had been distracted. Now, in relief, his face was bright and relaxed. He began to rub her belly slowly, knowing exactly where and how, having already been through two pregnancies with this woman. Her heart constricted with remorse and shame at how she had tricked him, but then set with determination. She reminded herself, we have no one to see here. As his hand moved over her belly, she again remembered her dream.

Gaius smiled lazily. 'Yes, you may go now and again to this Modron or whatever her name is, accompanied by Marcus, not Telemachus.'

She smiled up into Gaius's face. 'Our baby will be beloved and powerful, in Rome, in Batavia and in Britannia.'

What did she mean by that? he wondered. No matter. Enough talk for one day. 'Good night, my dear,' he said, and left the room to work a few hours more.

5 NO ARGUMENT

THE NEXT DAY

After breakfast, Marcus faced his father. He knew he was in trouble. But why shouldn't he be allowed to travel south, just for a few miles? There were forts all along the road with hundreds of soldiers. All the trouble came from the north, beyond the Wall. Besides, he was not a baby to be cooped up and coddled at home all the time. Bran was his friend and he would take care of him! Marcus's manner was determined, calm, but a note of grievance – even independence – sounded in his voice.

'So we rode all morning and ate lunch by a river. And then we rode over a tall ridge of hills, hardly a mountain, but big,' he said, looking around the table at his family. 'And then we came to the earthworks. They are amazing, Father,' he said.

Gaius made no reply. Marcus glanced at his mother, but she too said nothing. A bad sign. Suddenly he didn't want to tell them about Cartimandua's house or the huge enclosure with its high stone-and-earthwork walls. He skipped that and went on with his story.

'We slept out and then the next day we rode back, going a slightly different way, through a lot of Brigantian settlements, Father.' The air stayed thick around the table. 'Their Celtic language is impossible for me to follow. I know people from Gaul might be able to understand them, but not I. Maybe after some time here I could learn it. But every settlement we came to,' he said with a serious, helpful voice, 'the men were sitting in clusters talking – with great energy. I made out one word, Father, because I kept hearing it, in settlement after settlement, but I decided it was best not to ask Bran what it meant.'

Silence.

'It is really impossible to pronounce, so I won't be getting it right, but it's something like "rrrrruvel". You see, you have to roll that first bit so you sound ...' He was about to laugh when his father looked up suddenly, stared right into Marcus's eyes, and barked the most violent, frightening sound at him that Marcus had ever heard.

'Into my study. Now!' Before the sense of the words could invade and occupy Marcus's alarmed wits, his father was up and moving rapidly. Marcus jumped to follow him, leaving a pale mother and older brother.

'Mother, I can't stand this,' Telemachus whispered, as soon as they were gone. 'Last night was awful, and now this already this morning!'

'Be quiet. You'll stand whatever you have to. Marcus never should have gone so far without permission, unaccompanied by an adult, in a frontier district,' she said sternly. 'I don't know what the word he overheard meant,' she added, almost to herself, clearly worried for her younger son.

Telemachus turned and looked long and hard at his mother. He had been as upset by his own conduct last night as by his father's. He needed to understand what was happening in their family. No one was behaving normally. His mother was very quiet, his father explosive, his brother defiant, and he rude and insulting. What was working on their nerves?

'Mother, were we right to have left Rome?' He tried to keep his voice calm and reasonable, unlike last night, to show her he could control himself.

'Telemachus, you forget yourself. You are not head of this family and I do not owe you an explanation for my decisions. We are together as a family. That is enough.'

As she had watched him last night, and now at breakfast, she saw that Gaius was right, that the time had come to send Telemachus away, to allow him to finish his studies, start his career and grow up. There could not be two adult males under one roof, she thought wryly.

'Telemachus, it is time you began your career and had a bit of independence. As you know, your father proposes sending you to Rome, to live with his brother, Flavius Aurelius Rufinus. He has done extremely well and one day he may even become the Praefectus Aegypti. He will help you to become a good administrator and soldier, able to rise through the military ranks.' She smiled at her handsome son. 'Perhaps one day you will have a procuratorship.' She looked directly at him for a moment, to read his inclinations, then looked away and down, to allow him his privacy. He has become a man, she thought.

Telemachus was silent. These ideas were not new to him. Once he had yearned for the *toga virilis* ceremony. That seemed childish now. Rome, a career, beckoned him. He had been dreaming of it for weeks. Then the thought of Rhiannon filled his mind. His face relaxed when he remembered Modron's warning about boys. He heard again, 'I'll tell you what I want. I want to know where the Military Road leads.'

'I will consider what you say, Mother. Thank you.'

He looked now – for the first time in weeks, it seemed – at his mother. She had just begun to move as a pregnant woman does and he wondered why he had never thought to ask how she felt about this pregnancy. Her first-born might be off to Rome and Marcus was growing up. With her boys just leaving childhood, she, however, would be starting again, unable to leave, committed for years to the edge of Empire. Did she want another baby? Did she want to give birth here? The memory of his grandmother flashed through Telemachus's mind. His mother would be alone, without female family members for the first time. He had been selfish, hadn't thought about his mother at all. Now he saw she looked weary and sad. Full of contrition, he asked, 'Mother, are you all right? Are you pleased about the baby?'

'I don't quite know how I feel, Telemachus,' she said quietly. 'I'll just have to see. But I do know how I feel about my boys. I'm pleased with you and want you to continue learning and maturing. Marcus, in general, seems fine and is the right age to stay up here with me, at least for a few more years. I have been –' she now looked directly at him – 'very

160

pleased for us all to be a family again. I missed your father. And up here I think I will like it.' She felt her belly. 'This child is the start of our new life in Britannia. Our own "Brittunculus".' She smiled as she used the slang nickname the Roman legionaries gave to the natives, the 'wretched little Britons', but her reasonable words and little joke did not wholly reassure Telemachus. He saw she was concerned. However, he saw behind that that she was strong, with a love of life and a will to live fully. She will be all right, he thought, and smiled back into her eyes.

Just as Telemachus began to smile, into the room came Gaius. He had a different air now, one that they recognized as military. 'No one leaves the fort without my permission. The word Marcus overheard is Celtic for "revolt".'

PART THREE

WARM BLOOD

A fox and a wolf curled up together, for warmth, in a bed of bracken. The soldiers had already been through the field to gather flooring for their fort. Had they seen these two animals sleeping side by side, they would not have believed their eyes.

The fox and the wolf had been hunting. Evidence of a lamb dinner still showed on their teeth and paws.

'The warm blood is rising in our lovers,' drawled the regal fox.

The wolf smacked his lips, savouring a last morsel of food. 'Oh, Queen, how sad. One couple will be so happy and one so miserable.'

'How feeling you are,' said the fox, eyes glittering with laughter. 'A lamb in wolf's clothing.'

Tightly shutting her eyes, the queenly fox stretched the full length of her body, revealing a slightly rounded tummy and little white paws. 'I could sleep all day in the lovely autumn sun. The soldiers will not return. When it is dark, we will scout north of the Wall.'

The wolf lifted his head and perked up his ears. 'Around the farm of Peredur and Macha, perhaps?'

'A wolf should enjoy that chase,' purred the fox.

The wolf smacked his lips and seemed to smile. He stretched, crossed his paws before him and nestled his head down to sleep.

6 THE PARADE

ANCIENT MYSTERIES IN THE STABLES

Though anxiously anticipated, war did not come, not in the following weeks. There was tension along the Wall and the *contubernia* who patrolled the northern stretches departed nervously each morning and returned gratefully each evening. News from the scout forts, Blatobulgium and Banna, brought constant assurances of war-readiness, but no hints of battle. The last open conflict had been ten years ago, when Modron's husband had fought and died. Ten years of skirmishes only had followed. Everyone felt the build-up for war, but who would start it and where? No one wanted to fight in the winter when the cold and wet were as deadly as any weapon. The limitless blue skies were giving way to grey and black cloud banks that scuttled furiously across the heavens, threatening snow and freezing rain. Gaius and Quintus began to wonder if a spring offensive was more likely. Still, for now Gaius insisted that his own family stay within Vercovicium's walls.

Being confined to Vercovicium was torture for the boys. Occasionally, the weather could surprise, bringing warmth and the last faint traces of summer. Though the leaves were turning bright colours and falling, bees swarmed dozily and the mossy ground gave off a pleasing bittersweet scent. Marcus was desperate to see Bran, and Telemachus, in a trance of misery, to see Rhiannon, despite his father's orders. Then fate came to their aid. Gaius decreed that a full military parade would be held on the first day of November. He wished to dedicate a new altar to Mars Cocidius, in honour of the union of the auxiliaries from the Empire's provinces and the fighting men of Rome. He wished too to give thanks for the fertility of his union with Claudia. Departing soldiers would be honoured, citizenships awarded, a new centurion appointed and a cockerel sacrificed.

The boys understood their father's purpose. The main point of such a parade was to thank the gods and try to ensure their favour. But it was also for the men, to allow everyone to be impressed by the overwhelming power and efficiency of the Roman military machine. Such shows raised morale among the troops, awed the locals, sent out warning signals to antagonistic tribes and dangled before the lads in the crowd the glamour of a career as a Roman auxiliary. The audience would be filled with the men's families – unofficial wives, sisters, mothers and children. This was their chance to see their men in all their power and pomp. Sons would dream of growing up and one day joining their father's unit. The grand display also took the men's minds off the approaching winter. The fort had one week to prepare and was in organized pandemonium.

The boys watched the preparations and made their plan.

They asked their mother if Modron, Rhiannon and Bran might be invited to view the parade. They knew the answer would be yes as the parade grounds were close to the fort and south of Vercovicium, making nonsense of a refusal. They suggested that the family arrive early in the morning. That way Claudia and Modron had plenty of time to examine the woven materials Modron had ready to show her and to discuss orders for cloth. Meanwhile, the four 'children', as Telemachus had said with an arch smile, might enjoy looking about the fort and watching the men practise for the parade.

Claudia looked long and hard at Telemachus when the two boys stood before her with their proposal. It had been a while since he had referred to himself as a child. Still, she could see no direct harm in the plan and agreed. She was eager too to get together with Modron, for herself and for her cloth. Brigit had been her only companion since Gaius had ordered them to remain inside Vercovicium a month ago.

Claudia thought of Brigit. Such a puzzle, that woman! Deep down, Claudia still did not trust her. Something was not right in the woman's heart. She had all the airs and graces of a Roman lady, but was also somehow prickly, ill at ease with her identity as a Brigante. Claudia felt, rather than understood, a danger lurking in Brigit and so never quite let down her guard. Brigit, in turn, sensed she was not trusted and resented it, Claudia knew. She is kind and cheerful, Claudia thought, and without her I would have gone mad these five months. But still Claudia was uneasy.

Maybe the display on the parade ground will please her, she thought.

The boys had counted on their mother's approval. Their plan was reasonable and they had read their mother's mood and mind correctly. To see another woman and samples of woven cloth would fully engage her. Gaius's command that they did not socialize with the locals still stood, but he allowed it to be softened on this one day.

So up the road through the *vicus* on the cold, bright morning of 1 November came Modron, Rhiannon and Bran, all grinning with anticipation at seeing their Roman friends. Bran had grown furious that early morning waiting for his mother to select and pack all her cloths and for Rhiannon to decide which tunic, leggings, shawls and cape to wear. Then she had to decide about the jewellery. Then she began combing and fluffing and braiding and un-braiding and partially braiding her hair. 'Rhiannon!' he had yelled. 'What is the matter with you? Hurry!' He was ready to hit her in his frustration, but Modron tapped him on the head with her shuttle to remind him to be patient. He scowled at them both and waited outside the roundhouse in the freezing November dawn.

The four friends greeted one another at the door of the Praetorium and immediately left the adults. They ran, as though in prearranged agreement, out of the fort's south gate and turned west to the stables. Had they turned their gaze left, they would have seen the parade ground from the elevation of the fort. It was a perfectly flat field lying at the floor of the valley through which the cart road cut. The grass and moss surrounding it had been trimmed and rolled for the big day and now looked like one of Modron's tightest weaves. The actual parade ground had been covered, almost paved, with little pebbles. As the boys had hoped, the stables, though full with over a hundred mules and twenty horses, were empty of soldiers. They were all in their barracks, polishing their equipment and practising for the big day.

The four burst into the stables and threw themselves upon the piled hay, laughing. A horse stabled nearby looked up, surprised but not afraid.

'We're here! We're together! Marcus, you old cow!' And with that, Bran pounced on Marcus, flattening him into the hay.

Marcus, yelling and yelping and cursing, rolled and tossed a leg over Bran, pinning him while he shoved both of Bran's shoulders into the hay. Rhiannon raised her eyebrows in haughty disdain and lay back languidly into her part of the hay. Telemachus, who had been amused by the younger boys and about to join in their fight, saw Rhiannon settle back. Seeing her made him catch his breath, then blush, then curse. Why can't I just look at her without falling apart? Could it be, a little sarcastic voice in his mind answered him, that you've been living in a fort of eight hundred men for five months? He rested on his side, supported by his elbow, and pretended to observe the scene from a distance. He tried to look disdainful of the boys, who were still play-fighting.

'Boys!' Rhiannon said, slightly rising. She had already

had enough of their foolishness and, as it showed no indication of letting up, decided to drop her languid posture to yell at them. 'You are too noisy. Stop it!'

Marcus looked at her and remembered from his first day in the roundhouse how sharp her tongue could be. He glanced at Bran, who was sticking out his tongue at his sister, which seemed just about the right response. Marcus howled with laughter and belted into the next stall, head first. Bran whirled around and chased him, screaming something in his language which sounded so furious it made even the cool Telemachus laugh.

Rhiannon lay back down, fully aware of how her red cloud of hair looked against the hay. She stared straight up at the wooden rafters and tried not to think of spiders. She knew her profile would draw Telemachus, but was afraid her thumping heart would reveal her nervousness. So she sat up, as though she'd just casually changed her mind, and shifted her position to lean against a wooden beam. Telemachus didn't trust his voice – it could crack or squeak or simply give away his excitement – and didn't want her to catch him staring at her. So when she sat up, she found him deeply engaged trying to split a straw. Her shoulders slumped slightly.

Telemachus cleared his throat. He felt suffocated by their nervousness and knew he had to change the mood somehow. Marcus had told him that he'd heard Bran's family talking about stone circles. They really did interest him, so he decided that this was as good a topic as any. 'Rhiannon?' he began, 'tell me about the stone circles and cairns around here. I've seen cairns before, especially when we were passing through Gaul, but never a stone circle. Who made them and why? Do you know?'

She looked up, surprised and flattered. She loved the stone circles and knew everything there was to know about them, or everything that her mother and her relatives and neighbours could tell her. She was pleased he wanted to know. She was grateful too for the distraction.

'They were built by our people ages ago, long, long before your people ever even knew about my land.'

'Why were they built? I mean, how? I heard some of the auxiliaries talking about them and they couldn't understand how such huge stones could be quarried, much less moved and put into place.' He glanced over at her and smiled ruefully. 'Overhearing auxiliaries' conversations has been my only source of information and practising battle techniques with them my only social life, ever since . . .' he stammered to a halt, embarrassed.

Her expression showed she understood and sympathized. His heart melted. She saw the reaction and carefully carried on the topic, saying, 'They were quarried and set up so long ago that even we have forgotten how. My grandmother once told me that she thought the circle just north of the Wall had been there for thousands and thousands of full moons.'

She looked over at Telemachus. He was listening closely.

'As for what they mean, much of that knowledge has been lost too. But the stones do show us the holiest day of winter, and of summer. On those days, the sun rises directly over certain stones and shines into the circle, on to an altar. Many farmers I know swear they can tell when to plant or to harvest, depending upon the way the sun strikes the stones or how the moon rises or appears between or above them.'

She lowered her voice and was about to speak when she realized the two twelve-year-olds had silently crept back to join them. She looked suspiciously at them to see if they were mounting an attack but settled back against the beam when she saw they were quietly – fairly quietly – snuggling into the hay. Even the horse opposite them was solemnly regarding her.

'One of our tribe's wise men once told me that he believed the stones guided the falling stars.' She looked around at all three boys. 'He told me something else. Something wonderful and magical, and if I tell you you must promise to tell no one.'

Three nodding heads.

She wondered why she was making them promise. The wise man had never told her not to tell others. She had been very young, but even back then she had felt he was imparting something magical that must never be forgotten, something he was storing just with her for safekeeping. Now she was passing it on to others. He had been a very old man, one of the original warriors who had fought under Cartimandua. She suddenly remembered the glint of the gold torc he wore, hidden beneath his woven loose robe. It was a pleasure to remember him, she thought, with his tattooed chest, full of blue swirls, and his bristly moustache. It had been a long time since she had thought of him.

'He said there were stone circles and stone avenues and stone markers all over this island. He said –' here she hesitated, but then rushed on – 'the ancient people of all the tribes decided, ages ago, to rearrange the land so that it reflected the skies.'

'What do you mean?' Marcus blurted.

Telemachus frowned, waiting for more.

'They looked up and saw there were patterns in the sky made by the stars. These patterns moved throughout the planting, growing, harvesting and resting seasons. They decided . . .' She paused again, for this story seemed so huge as to be unbelievable. 'They decided to dig up the earth, to change the landscape, making ditches and mounds and flat surfaces, and then to place these huge stones in lines and circles to reflect the patterns in the sky. He said they made the island into a "sacred landscape".'

'Why?' Telemachus breathed, stunned by the audacity of the scheme.

'To control the skies,' she answered.

'How?' he challenged, incredulous but poised to learn something he hadn't known. A little sarcastic voice in his mind whispered, 'How much of your patience here is due to the girl? You'd never stand for such nonsense from a boy.' Be quiet, he answered, and listened to Rhiannon.

'By the way the people changed the land and placed the stones, the stars were seen to rise and follow certain avenues on earth. They knew where the sun and moon would go next. They knew when the star patterns would move. They knew when the moon would block out the sun.'

Complete silence. Telemachus looked solemn. He had never heard of such power before and had to think about it. For the first time he felt an obscure sense of the limitations of Empire. After all, the Romans only wanted to control the earth, not the stars and skies too.

'These stones control the skies?' Telemachus asked.

'Yes.'

She looked with huge round eyes at him. This was the most sacred knowledge of her tribe. It was imperfect, dimly understood, and now only useful as a way to remember when to plant and when to harvest. But this was the ancient knowledge, held without written record in the placement of those stones. She watched carefully as Telemachus listened. He had listened! Perhaps he was different from other boys. Oh, I know he's just thinking about me, about liking me, she conceded, but still, he did listen. We might one day be able to be together – in a way I would like. She looked up at him through lowered eyes.

Catching the look, Telemachus gave in to the little voice's sarcasm: you're right, he said to himself. I can't disentangle her beauty from her words. She could say anything to me right now and I'd believe her.

Rising, she offered a silent prayer to Epona, hoping again that she had done right to tell the boys. Even the way she stood up was different from the way they did. They all watched her. She crossed the stables to stroke the quiet, attentive horse.

The younger boys, slightly unnerved by her story of a sacred landscape, tried to loosen the spell by simultaneously jumping up and shaking their bodies, like two dogs. That changed the mood and Telemachus rose.

'Bran and I are going down to the parade ground to see everyone get ready.'

'No, you aren't,' Telemachus interrupted. 'You know you and I have to dress for the parade. Mother is waiting for us. Bran can go with you, but you have to return now to the Praetorium.'

Marcus shot a look deep into Telemachus's eyes to make sure his brother was telling the truth. He was. So he swung his head over to Bran, nodded, and the two ran out of the stables, turning right, before Rhiannon knew what was happening.

'Marcus!' Bran called as they ran. 'Why do you think all those farmers are coming to the parade? Look, there are scores of them.' He pointed to the fields to the west of Vercovicium.

Marcus looked, then stopped and searched the vista. Bran stopped running too, waiting for Marcus's explanation.

'There aren't any farmers there, Bran,' Marcus said quietly, holding Bran's eyes with his. 'There aren't any farmers there, not that I can see – this time, anyhow.'

They both knew that Bran had, like Marcus, somehow seen something that wasn't there.

'What does it mean, Marcus?' Bran asked, scared.

'I don't know. But as you once said, they aren't hurting us. We'll just have to see.'

The boys looked at each other, both sighed and then began again to run back to the Praetorium.

Meanwhile, gathering all the courage and determination born of hours of dreaming, Telemachus walked right over to Rhiannon, who was now standing, slipped his arm around her waist, and quickly and gently kissed her on the lips.

She looked into his eyes – as Marcus had just done, though for a very different purpose – and stretched up for a second kiss.

'What's this?' boomed an auxiliary, turning round the corner. He was carrying a buckle and belt. 'Lovely day, isn't it?' he shouted, smiling, and walked right past them into the stables. 'Good thing I happened by this morning . . .' he yelled back at them, 'and not the Prefect!' A moment later he reappeared, carrying a buckle. 'I'm off then! Carry on!' And he swung out of the stables, went back around the corner and disappeared.

They were mortified. Dropping arms, sliding apart, heads lowered, cheeks bright pink, they slowly walked away from the stables but did not turn right. Anything to avoid that man. In silent agreement, they walked straight on, turning left at the next barracks block, right down the hill and, taking the most circuitous route possible, eventually ended up at the Praetorium in time for Telemachus to change for the parade.

THE PARADE

The crowd had arranged itself along three sides of the parade ground against the upward slope. Word had spread that Vercovicium was holding a full dress parade, so people had come from east and west, north and south.

The parade ground was some distance from Vercovicium and below it, so the spectators would be able to see the marching troops descend the slope, coming down the curving path that started at the fort and ran through the *vicus*. Everyone was straining for a good view, but order was maintained by the *duplicarii*, who ran along the four edges of the parade ground keeping people back. The parade wouldn't take very long, but in those few minutes the people would see nearly eight hundred men dressed in shining armour, helmeted, with sharpened, finely balanced weapons, marching in perfect unison. By now, three generations of Brigantes had grown up under Roman rule and had come to delight in these martial displays.

Whispers began to circulate through the crowd: 'The Prefect's family has taken its place!' Necks were craned as men, women and children strained to see the north side of the grounds. There stood the tribunal, a platform made of cut stones identical to those from which Roman forts and the Wall, milecastles and turrets had been built. Beside it had been erected the cohort's altars, including the new one, covered with a cloth, that was to be dedicated today. Sitting behind the altars, near the north-west corner of the grounds, was the Prefect's family, elegantly dressed, fixed and solemn in their dignity. Telemachus and Marcus had made sure that Modron, Rhiannon and Bran had places immediately behind and to the east of them, directly behind the platform.

The ground began to shake. Excitement spread through the crowd and heads swivelled to find the source. Marcus shot a smile at Bran, who smiled back. They loved this. This was Bran's first parade, despite his having lived so near Vercovicium. Marcus discreetly pointed to the ground and Bran nodded in delight. The parade grounds' small stones now hopped with each step as the mighty army approached. Out from Vercovicium, down through the *vicus*, across the causeway and over the cart road came the marching soldiers of the First Cohort of Tungrians.

The Prefect took the few steps up the tribunal and faced the empty parade ground before him. Behind him, at ground level, stood his adjutant, the *cornicularius*, and his cohort staff. The ground continued to shake, jumping to the thud of hundreds of men. The crowd looked first at the immobile Prefect, whose authority seemed to hold back the very clouds in the vast November sky, then to the cohort bearing down upon them. It was terrifying. Modron and Rhiannon clasped hands. Even though they knew this was a display, not a battle, they were overwhelmed by the power of the men marching in unison. Rhiannon felt faint with excitement but nodded that she was fine to her mother's quick, worried glance.

First on to the parade ground came the senior

centurion, Quintus Valerius. Behind him marched the cohort signifier, carrying the *vexillium*, a red cloth flag; then came the *imaginifer*, bearing a relief in gold and silver of the Emperor Hadrian; then the signifiers of the centuries, each bearing the *vexillium* of his own century. Quintus Valerius wheeled smartly and took his position in the eastern section of the ground. The unit's *vexillium* and the image of the Emperor were held aloft, one behind the other, immediately to his right. Each centurion took up position, in a line, to the senior centurion's left. They planted their pole ends into the pebbles and held forth their flags with rigid arms.

Led on by the inexorable pounding of the marching men, the cohort right-formed on to the parade ground. The first century right-formed next and came to attention, in rows of four, behind the first centurial standard. Then the second, third, fourth, fifth, sixth, seventh and eighth. From the moment the parade began in Vercovicium, the march had thundered its rhythm. Now it suddenly stopped. Silence. Rhiannon looked up into the sky, to see if the world would split.

Out came Quintus Valerius, who dressed the parade by the right. The men rapidly perfected their alignment with the unit *vexillium* on the far right. Once the parade was dressed, the senior centurion marched to the tribunal and reported to the Prefect. He halted in front of his commander, drew his sword to salute and spoke: 'Prefect, the First Cohort of Tungrians with eight centuries and seven hundred and fifty-two soldiers is drawn up, awaiting your inspection.'

Gaius returned his salute, listened and then descended from the tribunal to march along the front rank, accompanied by Quintus Valerius. He periodically checked soldiers' equipment and spoke to the men. All stood at attention, turning their heads to follow him along the line. The soldiers were in their finest uniforms with full body armour, helmets with plumes, swords and, in their right hands, *hastati*, points vertical with the poles resting on the ground by their right feet. Their shields were slung on their backs at the left rear and were held by straps. The centurions had no *hastati* but carried drawn swords. The armour glistened in the cold sun, and the size and physical condition of the soldiers could not fail to impress as they formed an iron wall, four men deep.

When he reached the end of the line, Gaius turned to face Quintus Valerius, who saluted. Gaius returned the salute and marched back to the tribunal, while the senior centurion moved to the centre of the parade and faced the men. He gave the command: 'Form around the tribunal in close order.'

The wings of the cohort moved forward and turned in to surround the tribunal on three sides. Centuries one and two made up the east side, three to six the south and seven and eight the west. Once the soldiers were in position, Quintus Valerius called out, 'Ready, Prefect.' Gaius then called, 'Cohort, rest.' On this command, the centurions sheathed their swords, the soldiers lay their *hastati* at their feet and all relaxed, looking up at the Prefect on the tribunal.

Gaius spoke: 'Soldiers of the First Cohort of Tungrians,

you hold the position of honour. You are the iron bulwark of our august Emperor Hadrian. Soldiers hold their shields in their left hand, exposing their right side. Only the greatest warriors are assigned "the right of the line", to protect their comrades. You are "the right of the line". Great of stature and mighty in strength, you stand here, as your forefathers stood at the battle of Mons Graupius. You are proud warriors of Rome and true representatives of your martial race. This is a great day. Every two years the family of the cohort meets together to remember past glories and to dedicate ourselves anew to the glory of Rome and to the future triumph of our arms. There are many veterans here today in the crowd, some indeed your own fathers, who watch you with pride and bless you as their true successors. By dedicating your lives to your fellows and the spirit of the cohort, you will always overcome the Brittunculi, who lack order and dedication. Mars Cocidius looks down and is well pleased to bless such a worthy body of warriors. Shortly, I will dedicate a new altar to renew our bond with this bountiful god.'

The adjutant then handed Gaius a scroll listing the soldiers who, after twenty-five years' service, were now retiring and here received citizenship for themselves and their children, and the right of legal marriage. Rhiannon looked about the crowd and saw happiness on many women's faces. Gaius gave each man a diploma. Then he turned to a retiring centurion and announced, to the delight of the century, that one of their own men, Optio Gnaeus Afranus, son of Bassus, was to come forward to replace him.

181

'Receive your sun-plumed helmet and cane of office from your predecessor and then take his place on the parade in command of the sixth century. You will present yourself at the first watch tomorrow to be sworn in by me as a centurion of this cohort.'

After another short ceremony at which the new recruits slipped into line to join their centuries, Gaius approached the new altar and said, 'On behalf of the cohort, I dedicate this altar to Mars Cocidius. May the god look upon his unit with favour, and protect, strengthen and support us.'

He then unveiled the altar and held up a pure white cockerel, its wings and feet tied. The crowd could see its head swivel and undulate. Gaius took up a dagger from the altar. As he drew the dagger across the bird's neck, red blood pulsed down its white-feathered breast. A clean kill. The soldiers and crowd were satisfied: this would bring good luck.

Then Gaius shouted, 'Good fortune to the First Cohort of the Tungrians!' and the soldiers roared out the same words to him. He placed the bird on its side on the altar and climbed the steps to the tribunal.

The senior centurion reported to him, 'Prefect, may I have your permission to re-form the cohort and march past in salute?'

Gaius answered, 'Yes, please, Centurion. And order a hundred and sixty *modii* of beer, twenty to each century, at my expense, to celebrate our rededication this night.'

As the centuries marched past the tribunal, Gaius saluted the standards with his sword and the centurions held out their swords in reply. The soldiers, as they passed, turned their heads to the right to look straight at their Prefect. When the last century had passed the tribunal, the centurion of the eighth century started to sing the marching song of the cohort. After he had finished the first line, all the soldiers joined in and sang as they wheeled left and marched back up the hill to the fort.

Bran looked down to see the pebbles jump again with each thudding step. He then gazed before him, seeing and hearing nothing. His body juddered with every step of the cohort, but his face was solemn. He had seen a display of power and precision and authority that was unknown in his life. He had seen the majesty of the Roman military machine and his life had changed forever.

THE FARM

After the parade, Brigit returned home to her cousins' farm, exhausted. This had been an extraordinary day. It began with Modron's visit, when she and Claudia pored over Modron's different woven fabrics and placed orders for many lengths. Then came the parade, which Brigit had been very excited about and had been expecting to enjoy. As a child and young woman in Rome, she used to go to all the spectacular displays of the Empire's might. She loved to go to the Colosseum, to see the chariot races and games, but was especially thrilled by the triumphant legions when they marched through the city.

Perhaps the day already had a touch of winter's cold, but

somehow she had not been moved by the parade and had even felt angry at Gaius and his men. First, she had been made to stand with the crowd and not, of course, sit with the family. She understood that, but it was uncomfortable for her. After all, she hardly belonged in the crowd. Then, perhaps because she knew Gaius so well in his own home, she was irritated by his dignified, impenetrable stance. He set himself up on that tribunal like a god! All those men – hundreds of them – parading past him with smartly turned heads, displaying their *hastati* and standards, the centurions holding out their swords. She could have laughed. She saw how impressed Modron and Rhiannon had been, and how Bran nearly swooned with the majesty of it all. Well, she had had a long enough day and was glad to return to the farm.

She entered the front door of the rectangular stone building and turned to face the shrine. She bowed before a small stone relief of the goddess Brigantia. Gentle thankfulness filled her heart. This was her goddess, her tribe, her people, more even than her kinsmen near Eboracum. She felt herself to be, from ancient lineage, of these hill people. As a little girl in Rome, Brigit had always dreamed about living in the shadow, under the influence, of her namesake goddess. Now here she was.

She gazed at the stone relief. In it, Brigantia wore Minerva's symbol of the Gorgon's head on her breast. She was crowned and carried a spear and the globe of victory.

Brigit began to pray: 'O High One, Exalted One, healer, protector of my tribe, fertility spirit, promoter of the welfare of lambs and cattle and patron of the crafts of smithing, dyeing, weaving and brewing.' She felt her jagged nerves calming. Every time she bowed before her patron goddess, she felt soothed, cleansed and loved.

Just then her cousin Macha called to her from the farm's kitchen. 'Brigit, is that you? Come, we have a visitor!'

Brigit stiffened. All the calm left her. She was back in reality, living in a stone house north of the Wall, obedient to her cousin's call.

She walked through to the other ground-floor room and saw Macha, her husband, Peredur, and another man who was unknown to her. He was older, fit, tough, with a bristling moustache and lines around his eyes and down the sides of his mouth. The sun had coarsened and burned the skin on the back of his neck. Seeing him, Brigit had an immediate physical reaction. She felt her stomach clutch and her heart race. Why should she feel this way? Surely this man was too old to be attractive, much less eligible. There was something about him that frightened her. She had flushed and now paled. Macha indicated that she should sit, for they were about to eat.

'So you've switched over from sheep to cattle, have you?' the stranger asked Peredur.

'Mostly. We always keep sheep, but . . . the forts pay well for the beef.' Peredur was ill at ease and the women understood why. Brigantes were famous for their herds of sheep and goats, but now, for money, they were rearing more cattle, as the Romans preferred beef.

So, Brigit thought, this stranger doesn't like the Roman presence.

'And are you so well off, then, that you can keep the cattle – keeping them on the grazing lands the sheep might have used – just so you can sell their milk and later slaughter them for their hides?' The stranger was pushing Peredur, staring into his face. No food had yet been offered and the men had only pottery tankards of beer.

'Yes,' Peredur answered, looking directly back. He resented this questioning.

'You've even started the Roman practice of growing hay, have you, to feed the Roman-bound cattle during the winter?'

'I have, Stellos, but I also grow wheat, barley, oats, hemp and flax, and raise plenty of sheep and pigs, just as in the old days. Yes, you'll find we've changed with the times, but we haven't forgotten the old ways,' Peredur concluded.

'Changed with the times ...' Stellos repeated and looked down. Suddenly, he looked up and straight at Brigit. She was thrown by the intense blue-white of his eyes and the force of his personality. 'Do you change with the times, or are you loyal to the old ways, Brigit?'

How did he know her name? Who was he? Brigit glanced at Macha, whose face gave nothing away. This man is making Macha anxious, but he is important to her – and to Peredur, she thought. Why? She looked quickly at him and liked his face. He was powerful, but attractive as well. She couldn't think how to answer him, so she sat silent. After all, which ways *did* she keep?

'My name is Stellos. Your cousins told me your name,' he said, smiling.

She nodded, embarrassed. Macha shot a look at her and saw everything. The men knew too. Here was a woman still hoping for marriage and children, vulnerable to the attentions of men. Stellos gave her a hard, long look.

'You work at Vercovicium, as companion to the Prefect's wife.' His tone was neutral, but his voice was deep and resonant.

She nodded again.

'Well, can you speak, woman, or are you mute?' he roared.

She started but then sat straight and answered boldly, 'I can speak and do not like to be barked at.' She put up her chin and, trying not to be too haughty but still to command respect, asked, 'Are you from around here? I don't recognize you.'

Stellos smiled slowly in response. 'No, you wouldn't. I'm from far west. My people are the Novantae. I've known your cousins for years and have stopped by.'

The Novantae! Brigit was stunned. She tried not to show it. 'Will you stay with us for a few days?'

Stellos was watching her carefully. 'Perhaps. Would that be all right with you?'

'Of course.'

'And then perhaps I might tell you about my people and how we live north of the Roman Wall, free of the Roman ways, not –' and here he glanced at Peredur – 'changing with the times.'

'That would be of interest,' Brigit primly replied.

The others exchanged a silent understanding.

'Come and help me to get the food, Brigit,' Macha said quietly, rising, and Brigit followed her.

Macha served breast of mutton, grilled over hot embers, with nettles, sorrel, dandelion and thistle boiled, chopped and tossed in butter with salt. She knew how to present a more Roman meal, but purposely chose to please their tribal-minded guest. Stellos spoke of the land, of loving it, of having had it in the clan for thousands of years. Everything he said rang true to Brigit. He is a protector of our tribal lands, she thought. Never mind that his tribe is Novantae and ours Brigante; he will look out for us too. He wants to reclaim our land, she suddenly realized. Immediately, she suppressed this thought. It was too shocking, too disloyal to Claudia and her family, and to all Brigit loved of Rome. No, no. She pushed the idea down.

When they had finished eating, Stellos rose and said, 'Brigit, would you care to walk with me in the night air?'

She was dumbfounded. As he stood above her, imposing, overwhelming, she was excited and scared. What did her cousin think? She looked in surprise at Macha, who just shrugged. Peredur was looking at Stellos.

Brigit was bewildered by Macha's seeming indifference and embarrassed by Stellos's invitation. She needed guidance. Was it wrong to go walking in the night with a Novantae warrior? What was he offering her? She looked at them blankly.

Peredur spoke: 'Our gods are for us. Brigantia, your namesake, is our protector. That's why we have her image in our house. What other people do or say is their own business.' He looked hard at Brigit and rose, while Macha began gathering and scraping the plates.

To the top of her mind floated the image of her bronze hand-mirror, the one she had inherited from her mother, she from hers and she from hers. She remembered the basket-weave effect of its decoration, giving the surface the look of a hidden face. She thought, am I that hidden face? I am a Brigante, she answered herself. I am Brigit, devotee of Brigantia, protector of my tribe.

'All right,' Brigit said, and rose.

PART FOUR

REVELATION

The dew cried out to the winter mist, 'Be still, for once, and listen to your queen.'

Gurn hovered in the air, floating, shifting. 'What is your wish, my sovereign? To conceal or reveal? I am, of course, expert at both.' As he whistled these words, icicles formed on the coats of animals, who snorted as they pawed the cold, hard ground.

'It is time we appeared to Marcus and Bran,' the dew commanded. 'They are ready.'

The mist swirled uneasily, mixing with the tiny exhalations of breath of the smallest field mouse. The dew hardened to frost. High above, the sky was huge and dark, full of the coming winter.

7 KIDNAPPED

WINTER DANGER AND DESIRE

The weather was unlike anything Telemachus and Marcus had ever experienced. It was so cold, windy, snowy and wet that they seriously thought, many times, they might freeze to death. They had not seen their friends, or anyone else apart from auxiliaries, servants, Brigit and the family, since the parade. Claudia took pity on them and asked Grumio to find them a companion.

One day, as the boys sat with their tutor, Titus Helius, listening to him lecture on 'the rage of Peleus's son, Achilles', Telemachus suddenly threw his scroll across the room and struggled to his feet, stiff and sore from sitting in the cold room on the cold floor. 'I'll tell you what rage is. And it isn't from having my slave girl taken from me, or being humiliated by my commander, or dishonoured before my men. My rage is like a river of lava: the total boredom and frustration of being cooped up here, day after day, half the summer, all autumn and now into this disgusting winter! I am a volcano. Vesuvius is nothing compared to how I feel!' With that, before the astonished eyes of his brother and tutor, he kicked one of the wooden stools so hard and high that it hit the ceiling. He let out a howl of pain, which brought the sudden appearance of slaves rushing from all corners of the Praetorium, dread on their faces. 'It's all right. Go. It's all right. Leave us!' Telemachus, bent over in undignified pain, waved them away with one hand while he rubbed his foot with the other.

Claudia heard the howl too and decided now was the time to bring in the companion Grumio had found. She ordered a slave to summon the old scout and the dog. The gales blew hard at her window, making draughts impossible to exclude, so she had constructed a fort of pillows around her on the chaise and now she lay there, beneath her cocoon of blankets, nourishing her 'pupa', as she liked to think. She shut out all thought of her angry sons as she waited for Grumio and dozed. A slave delicately placed another blanket, folded, over the top and back of her head to protect her further from the cold.

She thought about Brigit, how she always seemed to have some secret. I know she's spending some time with the children, which is a huge help to me. She distracts them a bit from this horrid cold winter. Perhaps my Brigit has some secret sin? A man I don't know about? She smiled. No, I don't think so. Surely she would talk about him, tell me about him. Still, that woman is not happy, Claudia mused. She is not fully at ease with me, or, I think, with Modron. She often seems afraid. But why should she be afraid? And I don't think she has been looking well lately. I wonder if I should raise this with Gaius, she vaguely worried, even as she began to slide again into contented and muzzy half-consciousness.

She was suddenly jolted by the scrabbling of feet on the stone floor and shouting from outraged slaves as they saw mud carried into the Praetorium, up the stairs and along the upper corridor. There was Grumio, beaming at her, oblivious of the tumult, and then, completely out of control, a rampaging, lurching, joyous puppy.

'Madam! Puppy dog! Yes, good? Good dog. Oh, yes. Big, strong! Oh, yes!' he bragged. 'There, there, darling. Shush. There, there. Good boy,' he whispered to the puppy, who was rapt in the bliss of where-am-I and what-is-this.

Claudia shook her head, then couldn't help but laugh. Slaves ran to unfurl her and, when she had risen, she led Grumio and the puppy out of her room and down the corridor to the study. They made slow but noisy progress as the puppy ran in circles around Grumio, tying up the old man's legs so he couldn't walk. Still, they did get to the study before the boys came out into the corridor, and Claudia had the pleasure of seeing their faces as the puppy bolted over to them, first leaping straight into Marcus and then Telemachus. Both boys rolled back, howling with delight, their legs crossed up against their stomachs as the dog jumped all over them, joyously barking.

Horrified, Titus Helius had immediately taken refuge behind his work table. Grumio continued to beam, deeply happy with the encounter. He had chosen the dog, he had 'trained' it, he had brought it for 'madam and the boys'. The puppy immediately sensed the pack's order: Telemachus, himself, Marcus, then Grumio. Claudia didn't yet figure, but when he did become aware of her, she would be top dog.

Helius abandoned all thought of teaching and gratefully accepted Claudia's suggestion that classes be dismissed for the day.

'Let's call him Nodens, the hunter-healer god!' Marcus shouted. 'He'll protect us everywhere, Mother!'

The boys laughed happily as they ran out of the Praetorium with Nodens. Claudia smiled appreciatively at Grumio, apologetically at Helius, and returned to her cocoon, saying, 'Well done, Grumio. You chose perfectly. He is as foolish as the boys.'

But even Nodens couldn't hold back the boys' boredom, which returned as the days continued pitch-black and freezing. The huge north wind blew and blew. Snow fell and drifted against all the buildings of the fort. It took ages to get warm by a fire, but less than a moment to feel frozen again when beyond its range. The boys had no one to see, no one to do things with. Marcus played all the time with Nodens, but sorely missed Bran. Telemachus was lost to dreams, either of Rome and his brilliant career as an administrator of the Empire, or of Rhiannon, the most beautiful girl in the world. He tried to weave these dreams together, so that his father, thunder-struck by his son's astonishing career, gave his blessing to marriage with Rhiannon. Then Telemachus would sigh. He had everything ahead of him, nothing begun. He had hardly even seen Rhiannon, much less proposed to her. His life seemed as dreary, bleak and slow as the winter outside the Praetorium's windows.

The legionaries and auxiliaries were busy and, when off duty, cross and cold; they had no time for the boys. No one believed war would come in winter. However, every single auxiliary and legionary with whom Telemachus spoke, as well as Gaius and Quintus, did expect trouble, somehow, sometime. It would come stealthily and be well planned to cause maximum damage. Huge battles would wait until spring, but short, violent bursts of fighting were overdue. In this tense atmosphere, the only relief, besides playing with Nodens, was the baths, but even then a person can have only so many baths. The boys decided to rebel.

Telemachus wanted to meet Rhiannon – anywhere – and Marcus, with Nodens, wanted to explore with Bran. So they decided to propose a secret outing to the stone circle just a mile or so directly north of their part of the Wall. Claudia had given permission to Brigit to be the carrier of notes between the two households. Although Gaius had been clear about the boys not socializing with the natives, Claudia decided no harm could come of a simple correspondence. She felt guilty for having taken them from their friends in Rome and wanted to help them at least exchange notes with the only friends they had here. Brigit had helped Rhiannon and Bran with their simple, written Latin and had double-checked that the replies of Telemachus and Marcus weren't too difficult for their friends to read. In this way, she learned of the plot for each twosome to spend the day together.

They begged Brigit not to reveal their plans, as they were desperate to see each other and were asking for only one outing. Brigit had changed over the autumn and winter, Telemachus and Marcus agreed. It was quite a complicated change. She was less eager to please, but seemed gentler. Although there were days when she seemed genuinely very happy, she struck them as basically more fearful than before.

The boys used to talk late into the night about the few adults in their lives: Gaius, an excellent Prefect and a much improved father, Claudia, muzzy and content, and Brigit, the official family friend. One night they were playfully arguing about Grumio, with Marcus maintaining he was a foolish gardener and Telemachus, who knew him better, insisting he was special. 'Oh, he's special, all right,' Marcus howled and bashed Telemachus with his pillow. The boys agreed that their parents' marriage had made it over the rough reunion and that their mother would not be returning to Rome – soon, anyway.

The thought of Rome reminded Telemachus of the next season, spring, when he was meant to be returning. Marcus knew he was excited at the prospect and envied him his future.

'I don't have any dreams, Telemachus,' he moaned. 'I mean, I don't know at all what I want to do when I grow up.'

'You aren't meant to know yet, simpleton,' he joked, lazily swinging his pillow near his brother's head.

'Yes, but everyone else knows what he or she is doing. Father is commanding the fort, Mother is having a baby, you will be studying with our uncle to become an administrator. What about me? I have a real friend, finally, after Rome, which is good, and I have a dog –' Telemachus snorted – 'and I see spirits.'

Telemachus immediately grew solemn. 'I don't think you should joke about seeing spirits, Marcus,' he advised quietly.

'I'm not joking. It is true,' he said, looking up for comfort to his brother.

'We shouldn't talk about it,' Telemachus returned. 'It's dangerous.'

Both boys fell silent. Telemachus didn't know what to think. Did his brother really see spirits? Marcus had told him earlier that Bran had seen them too, but he still wondered if that was just Bran being a good friend, trying to reassure Marcus. He breathed in, then out slowly, and glanced sideways at his little brother. Meanwhile, Marcus had given up looking for comfort and was just staring into the middle distance, waiting for Telemachus to continue.

'As for your other points, they'll all come clear with time. At least you aren't in love with a Brigante,' he said, returning Marcus's mournful look.

At that, they knew they had discussed all they could for the time being and so turned again, more practically, to plan their outing.

Brigit did not know the whole plan. She understood the four were to meet at the stone circle just after dawn on the appointed day, but she didn't know of Telemachus's intention to meet Rhiannon earlier, before the arrival of the younger boys. Unbeknownst to Brigit, Telemachus had quickly scribbled an extra line on the writing tablet, right under the proofread message. It had asked Rhiannon to come an hour earlier than the boys, and Rhiannon, when she replied, had simply written, 'Yes,' at the start of her first sentence.

CAPTURED

The day arrived. Telemachus hadn't slept a wink the long night before, just waiting for the first cock to crow. He slipped out of bed, but before he could dress, he heard someone walking towards his bedroom. Quickly, he jumped back into bed and pulled the blankets up to his head. It was his father!

'Telemachus, wake. I have a surprise for you,' he whispered, gently shaking his elder son's shoulder.

Telemachus pretended to wake and be baffled, pleased by his father's presence.

'I have watched you practise with the auxiliaries in the parade ground and I know you have been bored, cooped up in the fort. I have arranged especially for you to go out today with the Nervii patrol, on its route to Hawk Ridge. You leave before dawn, so get moving!' He grinned and slapped his son's posterior, delighted with his little surprise. He was pleased with himself, as a father and an administrator, to have seen and acknowledged his son's developing competence and to have rewarded him with an adult job. Of course, there would be eight other men riding with him, which was only reasonable.

Telemachus thought he would die. He lay like a dead man in his bed. His father's grin began to be replaced by a perplexed expression. 'Wake up, boy! Did you hear what I said? Get out of bed and move!'

Telemachus knew he had to go, had to pretend to be delighted, grateful even, had to miss Rhiannon, to leave her standing alone in the dark. His heart breaking, he turned a glad expression to his father and leapt out of bed.

Satisfied, Gaius called out, 'The senior soldier in charge is a good man. Obey him as if he were the Prefect,' and left him to dress.

A bit later, just after dawn, Marcus, also too excited to sleep, crept down to the kitchen and raided the larder, pulling out all kinds of food – stuffed dates, fried bread coated in honey, sweet wine cakes and honey cakes – bundled them up and, with Nodens, unobtrusively slipped through the fort's streets, like any boy with his dog. That the boys had been ordered to stay in the fort had been kept private, known only to the family, so as not to alarm an already tense cohort. Marcus had no trouble, striding along unchallenged. As for his father, Marcus knew he had a long strategy meeting scheduled with Quintus and the other centurions that would take all day.

In the early-morning light, Marcus and Nodens walked past the hospital of Vercovicium, then past some barracks and up on to the Wall near the north gate. Marcus had grown taller and more muscular during the year, yet even with his new size and bulk he still didn't attract attention; he was the youngest member of Vercovicium, accepted and then ignored as the Prefect's younger son. This neglect didn't bother him, for it enabled him to get away with a lot more than Telemachus ever could. That was the good side of not having a job or career or pregnancy, he smiled happily to himself.

Nodens was delighted with the plan. He ran along the Wall, barking at anyone and anything, frantically wagging his tail, poking his long snout up everyone's tunic and into any sack of food. He was a deer-hound and instinctively loved being outdoors. The cold, wet air excited him and he couldn't wait to escape the confined Wall walkway and run wild in the snow, over the fields and hills below and north of the Wall. They walked for about half a mile. Then, waiting until the watch had passed, they ran down the stone stairs and the diagonal mud path to the base of the cliff. They kept going quickly on the path, trying to get out of sight. He thought, Telemachus was right. No one can see me, or I them, in this dark. And it's already well past the break of day – whatever that means in this black world! It felt wonderful to be out and free and having another adventure with Bran. Having Nodens there too was perfect.

Marcus had no trouble walking rapidly straight north and finding the stone circle. Nodens pelted up the slope, but kept rounding back to check on his charge. The way was a steady ascent, completely cleared of trees by the legions – for better surveillance – with forests in the distance. Claudia had seen this upward-rolling countryside on her first day and been appalled to realize that the land did indeed keep going north. As they approached the circle, Marcus saw a slightly tilting megalith and heard Bran's warning call, that of the unsociable carrion crow. 'No one expects a crow to be in a flock,' he had once explained to Marcus. 'That way I can make the cry and no one is surprised not to see birds.'

Bran smiled in greeting. 'It worked! Here we are. It feels like years since we last saw each other,' he said. 'Let me have a look at this famous dog you've been writing about. Hello, Nodens!'

As soon as Bran saw the dog, he crouched down to rub his head hard. Nodens loved this and rolled on to his back, four legs to the sky, for a good tummy rub. Bran laughed and started to wrestle with the dog. Marcus joined in too. He held Nodens down and began rubbing his tummy so the dog's leg flexed frantically, making both boys laugh.

'Any trouble?' Bran asked eagerly.

'No,' Marcus happily replied. 'Perfect.'

'So where have Telemachus and Rhiannon gone, then?' Bran asked, interested.

Marcus froze and looked at Bran.

'What is it?' Bran immediately asked.

'Telemachus couldn't come. Our father woke him up and unexpectedly sent him on duty with the patrol. He couldn't explain to Father, of course, so he had to go! I heard about it as I was leaving.'

Bran was watching Marcus's face. 'Marcus, he had a plan with Rhiannon to meet her here, early, before we arrived.'

'I know! *He* knew! He couldn't wait to see her. He just couldn't tell our father, could he?'

'Rhiannon came here, to this circle, at dawn,' Bran quietly said.

'Where is she?' Marcus nervously asked, looking around the circle with its fourteen-foot diameter as though somewhere in this area a girl might stand unnoticed.

Both boys were silent. Then they began listening. Too late. From out of nowhere a band of men – raiders – came and grabbed the boys. They quickly gagged their mouths and tied their hands. The men spoke in rapid, whispered Celtic, bewildering Marcus. But Bran immediately began trying to speak around his gag, pleading and begging with them. It was hard to say how many men there were, as it was still dark, even at mid-morning. Marcus could see that they wore coloured, woven, woollen cloaks over dark tunics and leggings lashed on with leather strips. He looked down and saw sturdy leather sandals stepping quickly around them. He was aware of fear, strength, speed, danger. They and he were afraid, as was Bran. He saw a raider hit Bran, who immediately slumped over. I've been kidnapped by raiders, he thought, as a blow struck his head and he passed out.

IN THE RAIDERS' CAMP

Marcus awoke in a large wicker cage. He was terrified. He'd heard that the ancient Britons used to weave monstrous-sized wicker 'men' around their sacrificial victims and then burn them alive. Bran was slumped over in a similar cage near him. Nodens had curled up beside Marcus, his overhanging eyebrows giving his face an anxious expression. They were inside a deer-skin tent. Marcus's bundle of food was gone. He could hear and smell a roaring fire burning outside the tent. Inside, it was cold, dank and dark. Because the flaps were tossed back over the tent's top, some wintry sunlight got in. About twenty men were milling around the cages. Marcus was amazed at their ferocious appearance. Their trousers and cloaks were dazzling in their bright and contrasting colours. They looked unlike any men Marcus knew. It wasn't their facial expressions but the moustaches and beards that shocked him. The Emperor Hadrian had a beard and had made beards fashionable in the Roman world, but Roman beards were nothing like these. These are more like pelts, Marcus thought. The men's faces were sombre and intelligent, and their bodies very fit and hardened.

Marcus wasn't scared. Now he was angry with himself for making this disaster possible, worried for Bran, as he was a Brigante caught fraternizing with a Roman, and very sorry for his parents, who, when they heard, would be sick with worry. For his own situation, he was absolutely clear-sighted. He saw Bran make a movement. He was regaining consciousness. Bran looked about with dark, troubled eyes and spotted Marcus. He gave him a long stare, then began looking about the tent.

At the same moment, Marcus and Bran saw Rhiannon. She too was caged. Bran's reaction was to stiffen, to make himself absolutely still. The two boys exchanged looks but said nothing.

The men continued to move about the tent. The boys watched them while looking at Rhiannon. They didn't dare speak to each other. The men seemed to be getting ready to do something. Some were sitting on their cloaks on the ground, sharpening their daggers against a hand-held stone. Others were adjusting their sheaths by pulling out their swords and jamming them back in, then shortening or lengthening the straps. Men were bent over, retying the leather strips criss-crossed around their shins. Wooden shields with metal bosses were propped up against the sides of the tent. The boys could see a few had bronze trimming. Suddenly, in strode the most powerfully built of the raiders, an older man with a full head of hair and a moustache. He looked with piercing blue-white eyes at the three captives. He took in that they were conscious, but didn't say a word. Rhiannon moaned.

The powerful man shot a warning look at the boys. 'She's drugged,' he said in Latin. 'We gave her warm beer with crushed valerian root. She's waking.'

Rhiannon moved her head slowly from side to side, as though dizzy, but opened her eyes. She saw where she was. Then she saw the two boys. Her eyes grew huge, but like them she said nothing. Certain basic aspects of the situation were clear: they had been kidnapped, they were at their captors' mercy and talking would only reveal information. But there was another shock to come.

Into the tent came Brigit. She looked awful. Her black hair, always worn pulled back in a bun, was tousled and loose, hanging in her eyes and down her neck. She had huge dark circles under her red-rimmed eyes.

'Stellos!'

He turned, slowly grinning, to face her. 'You and I will speak in Latin for the benefit of the Roman.' He looked at the boys. 'Are you surprised that a barbarian,' he sneered, 'can speak Latin? We Novantae and Selgovae, over three generations, have had many dealings with your Empire. We understand all too well how your people work. Now it is time for a little revenge. Just a little, to soothe our pride.' He smiled slowly, showing long, yellow teeth through his beard. 'The Roman we will exchange for gold. The Brigante with his sister we will take to our lands as slaves.'

'No! That was not our plan. The Roman yes, the Brigantes no.'

'Our plan? Our plan?' he mocked, turning to share the joke with his men, who were watching closely and silently.

'Yes! Let them go!' Brigit beseeched. Her eyes looked into his, reminding him, and anyone else who looked on her, that there was something between them that gave her words weight.

'No, Brigit,' he replied, looking back into her eyes. For a moment, regret and a flash of shame flickered within his gaze. He allowed himself to soften enough to explain his logic to her. 'Even though she is friendly with Romans, this one of the red hair is strong and young and will make a fine slave, bear many children, help our people.'

Brigit's face collapsed.

Rhiannon's face became as inscrutable as a bronze mask. Her features seemed pounded out by hatred. Stellos turned to look at Bran.

'The boy is strong too. You Brigantes make healthy

children, even under foreign influence,' he said, smiling cruelly. 'He is young enough to come now under our influence, to become a powerful Novantae warrior.'

None of the children moved.

'And me?' Brigit asked. Her eyes bored into his, but there was no hope in them.

'What about you?' Perhaps if she hadn't asked, or had asked in a different way, with confidence and hardness, Stellos might have answered her differently. Perhaps if she had assumed absolutely that she was to be part of his future, part of the tribal war against the Romans, she would have stood differently, her face would have looked different, and there would have been no need for her to speak at all.

Instead, a little voice crept out, spoken to no one in particular. 'What will happen to me now?'

'That is not my concern,' Stellos replied, standing solidly before her.

'But ...' She looked about the room. 'I helped you. I told you where to find the Roman boys.'

Incredulity flashed across the three captives' faces.

'Boys? Boys? I see only one Roman boy. Where is the other?' Reminded of her failure, Stellos gave vent to his anger.

'I told you. It was unexpected. He was sent north with the patrol. I helped you. I acted as a true daughter of the Britons. I chose you ... I'm one of you now.' Brigit was beginning to be afraid. She had gathered up and thrown at him every possible bond she had hoped to share with him.

This man was her man, this tribe's cause was her cause. She had made her choice and had nothing more to give. All she asked in return was to belong.

'One of us? Ha! Never.' His face contorted with disgust. 'No one of the Novantae or the Selgovae, or even of the Brigantes of long ago, would betray as you have. How could I ever trust you? You betrayed your friend, the Prefect's wife, leading her children into a trap, humiliating her husband. You betrayed your relative, Modron, sending her children into slavery. You aren't one of us. You aren't one of them. You are nobody, nothing.'

Brigit's mouth was dry and she could not speak. The men stood back and waited for the *coup de grâce*.

'We have held a council and have decided to exile you. We exile you beyond the lands, beyond the Roman Empire. You are welcome nowhere. Everywhere you go people will repel and hunt you.'

'Kill me, then,' her dead voice answered.

'No.' He looked at her without pity, without interest.

The men circling her moved closer, in silent unison. She fell back another step. She looked into each impassive face, then back at Stellos, and finally into the three terrified faces within the wicker cages. What she had done, what was her punishment, came down hard upon her. With a wail, she whirled around and ran through an opening made in the circle, out of the tent and into the vast, unkind world.

Stellos now faced the three captives. Something was different here. Ah, he saw. The Brigantes were immobile, furious. The Roman was cool, distant. He approached

Marcus. Although the wicker cage was too small to allow Marcus to stand, he could sit upright. He raised his chin and looked up with an eerie calm into Stellos's face. Marcus burned with cold rage.

Stellos chuckled. 'It looks like we have three gaming cocks here.' The men laughed. 'A shame we can't set them upon each other for bets. But then –' he paused to look into the eyes of all three – 'I don't know which I'd bet on. Hatred is in all their eyes.'

'Stellos,' Marcus said. 'That is your name?'

Stellos nodded, smiling.

'Do you know of Longinius?'

Stellos's eyes narrowed but he did not reply.

Marcus continued: 'The Roman commander, friend of the Emperor Trajan himself, kidnapped by Decabulus, the Dacian king. Decabulus hoped Trajan would call off his invasion to save his friend. What happened, Stellos? Tell the men what happened. Tell them in your language.' Tension made Marcus's voice high, but even without understanding his words no one could mistake his bravery.

Now Stellos chose to speak. He did not translate but answered, 'Longinius killed himself, little bantam cock. Is that what you will do?' Stellos slowly smiled.

'And the Roman legions advanced, razed the Dacian capital, slaughtered everyone, even the new-born infants, and hunted down the king.' Marcus didn't blink.

Stellos licked his lips. 'We hate you Romans. We want you out of our land. You took our land, good, rich, farming land, and "gave" it to the weak Brigantes. We can't force you out, but we can torment you. We can kidnap the son of the Prefect and exchange him for gold. He won't fetch much, but the humiliation we will inflict makes the effort worthwhile.' He turned his head to share the pleasure with his comrades. They were watching their commander.

Seeing this watchfulness, Bran suspected it might be wariness. He spoke in Celtic, in a dialect common to his tribe and the raiders' tribes. 'Stellos! You put fellow Britons into cages. What is this? Is this the work of a great British leader, a patriot?'

Stellos regarded him silently. The men shifted.

'You capture children, and a girl! We Britons honour our women. Is life so changed for your tribes that you find glory in bringing dishonour to the Brigantes? Do you feel like men when you kidnap children?'

These shafts struck their mark. Stellos glared at Bran and moved threateningly towards his cage.

To insult Bran and disassociate him from the culture of his men, Stellos now spoke in Latin, emphasizing that Bran had switched over and betrayed his people. 'Brigante boy, how dare you call yourself a Briton? You are probably a half-breed, conceived in some ditch, from the loins of a Roman legionary and some Brigante. Cartimandua let in the Romans. She sold herself for Roman trade. She abandoned her people to the Empire, gave up their sovereignty and hid while the Roman legions ripped into our lands, laid their stone roads, their stone forts, their stone cities.' He leaned over towards Bran, blue-white eyes burning. 'They're everywhere now, Brigante boy. They shoved us north,

211

giving your tribe part of our land. Their Wall from the Otherworld cuts across the whole country, from sea to sea, trapping us, even stopping the wanderings of the deer and stags. Cattle and sheep are forced to know only the pastures on their side of the Wall. We will never get them out, boy. Never. And who let them in? Your queen, the sow of the Brittunculi!'

Bran thought he would spit at him now. But Stellos's words gave him an idea. Answering in his Celtic dialect, he said, 'Impious fool! How do you know Cartimandua's spirit does not haunt the countryside?'

Stellos ducked his head as though he had been hit. Everyone's face was transfixed with doubt. Bran saw his words had strongly affected Stellos, more than he expected. He also saw Marcus in rapt attention, trying somehow to get the drift of his words. Bran changed to Latin now so Marcus would understand. He drove his point deeper.

'The Romans spirited her away. After victory, she disappeared – maybe to live among her people on the east coast. No one knows what happened to her. But the *genii cucullati* know. It would not be good for you, would it, if her spirit roamed the land? Perhaps other Brigante spirits roam the land, informing her of your whereabouts. Who knows who the spirit world supports? Are you sure you and your men are safe?'

Marcus gazed at Bran in awe. Bran's confidence proclaimed that he knew exactly what he believed, why he resisted Stellos and what future he wanted for his land. He wasn't even afraid to invoke the spirits.

By now, Stellos had regained his balance and neither moved nor shifted his gaze. Boring deeper into Bran's eyes, he said, in dialect, 'Gurn supports us. This we know.'

Aggressive murmurings of assent were heard from the men.

Bran sat immobile but was frantically thinking. How could Gurn support this hopeless resistance to the Romans? How could Stellos claim he knew Gurn did? Bran had little experience standing up to a man, but he felt his confidence flow back.

With a brief apologetic glance at Marcus, Bran changed again to dialect, wanting to make sure the men understood. 'Stellos, you have no idea what Gurn supports.' Bran's young face squarely confronted Stellos's gaze. He was a child in years, but had grown up without a father and been made to be aware of the realities of a north Briton's life.

'You are a proud warrior,' he continued. Stellos looked surprised and wary. 'I think you are jealous and afraid. You know you will be just another farmer when the Romans administer your lands. Everyone is equal, governed by the same laws and privileges under Roman law. Novantae and Selgovae farmers and traders will grow rich. Yet you would rather terrorize them, desperately holding on to your power, and deny them access to the Empire. You're a bully, a cheat and a coward.'

Stellos grabbed the wicker cage and shook it, tossing Bran on to his side, where sharp straw cut his face.

'Shaking the cage, scaring a child, won't disprove the

truth of my brother's words, Stellos,' Rhiannon called out in dialect, scorning him. 'Look at your men. They heard my brother and they know he is right. You mock our queen, you insult our tribe. You have offended the Brigantes by stealing their children for slavery. You bring down the wrath of the Roman legions and auxiliaries by kidnapping their Prefect's son. The gods will revenge themselves upon you, Stellos. Your days and those of your band are numbered.'

As Stellos rose, his fingers twitching, to hit Rhiannon, a burst of noise filled the air. Everyone jumped to hear the sound of horses galloping up to the tent, neighing and snorting. In each man's face Stellos could read the question: 'Is this, so soon, the revenge the girl vowed?'

'Men! It is only our comrades. We will be fifty strong, with horses, spears, daggers and shields. We shall see who carries the day. Come! We will raid these Brigantian farms for horses and plunder. Take anything or anyone you want, but nothing that will slow you down. On to your horses, quick.'

The twenty men grabbed their weapons and ran out of the tent. Their worried expressions had been banished by battle-lust. Outside, they met their comrades, who had brought them their horses and, unknowingly, restored their determination and courage. They had been beguiled by the words of children! The raiders exchanged incredulous looks, laughed and mounted, ready to ride.

'You stay here, guarding these brats,' Stellos ordered one of his men.

'Shall I give them the crushed valerian root?'

Stellos narrowed his eyes. 'No, we may need to move quickly and I don't want to have to carry them.'

The man nodded and Stellos strode out of the tent.

'What's your dog's name, boy?' asked the wiry, hungry-looking raider. The man was tall and thin, his hair and beard straggly and unkempt, and his teeth yellow.

Marcus wasn't answering, so the man kicked his wicker cage. Nodens looked up, alarmed.

'He doesn't speak our language,' Bran shouted. 'The dog's name is Nodens.'

The man nodded slowly and said in dialect, 'A good name for a dog. No one knows what our god Nodens looks like. Did you know that? Sometimes we see him as a dog – maybe like this one. He protects and heals people in this life. Do you think this one will protect you? Do you know what's going to happen to you?'

He grinned yellow teeth at Marcus, who refused to look at him.

Not caring whether Marcus understood, but enjoying scaring the two Brigantes, the man continued in his dialect. 'Our Nodens leads the dead to the Otherworld. Will your Nodens do that for you, Roman boy?' He half pulled out his sword from its casing. 'Perhaps I should sacrifice you and your dog now to the gods, to appease the anger you all say Stellos has brought upon us.'

He turned his head to grin at Bran, but his gaze fell on Rhiannon.

'We'll wait a bit,' he whispered, forcing a deep look into

215

Rhiannon's eyes while he continued to draw his sword. He showed her the sword, slowly, then carefully placed it out of reach, but in front of her, and left to stand outside near the fire.

WARNING AND PREPARATION

Telemachus, meanwhile, had ridden north with the patrol, following the ridge that ran up from the Wall, through the forests and eventually into the tribal lands of the Votadini. They followed this ancient track, expecting to take about four hours to reach the summit at Hawk Ridge. They called in at various farms along the way, including Brigit's cousins', where they arrived about mid-morning.

Telemachus was glad to get there, as he looked forward to a pleasant welcome from the family of his mother's companion. Mulled beer and bread of barleymeal and oatmeal, moulded into a round flat bannock and baked slowly on a griddle over the fire, would be perfect on this freezing, desperately disappointing day. Telemachus told his comrades of his hopes and they, frozen too and generally miserable with their winter patrol duty, readily agreed to stop at Macha and Peredur's farm.

There were odd moments from the beginning. Peredur came out of the stone house and said nothing, just looked at the eight men and their horses. Telemachus smiled and called out a greeting, but got no response. He saw Macha pass by the open door, but she did not greet them, which surprised him.

'I saw Brigit for a moment this morning,' Telemachus tried again. 'It was very early in the morning! She was just arriving at Vercovicium and I . . . well, I explained to her that I would be riding with one of the patrols.' He watched Peredur's reaction and was bothered by his impassivity. What was going on?

Peredur just nodded, silently, and looked back at Telemachus.

'Well, we'll be moving off, then,' he ended quizzically.

Disappointed, the patrol rode away north, further from the Wall and into the forest surrounding the farm. A deep freezing mist had rolled in from the coast, making the day even more horrible than it had been. The soldiers pulled their capes around their necks and heads, and morosely urged their equally cold horses on.

Suddenly, out of the fog, they heard hoof beats. Rapidly gaining on them came a horse and rider. It was Macha! She looked wild, terrified. The soldiers and horses caught her terror and began moving jerkily, looking in all directions, the horses high-stepping and shying.

She called out to them, while her horse stomped and pranced beneath her, 'Telemachus! Flee! Flee! I risk my life to tell you. A raiding party of fifty Novantae and Selgovae have kidnapped Marcus, Bran and Rhiannon.'

Simultaneously the senior soldier and Telemachus shouted back, 'What? Where?' as the soldiers turned their horses around to return to the fort.

The turmoil in Macha's face deepened their alarm. Telemachus shot his eyes into hers. 'How do you know this?' he bellowed. He had his horse under control and had brought it over to hers.

Although her face was grief-stricken, she held herself bolt upright. 'Telemachus, this morning, this morning my cousin left as usual for the fort. Soon after her arrival you must have seen her. But then, unbeknownst to you, she left Vercovicium and returned here, distraught.'

Telemachus felt dread in the pit of his stomach.

'She threw herself on to the floor, sobbing, and confessed to me and Peredur what she had done.'

He, the men and the horses were silent as she spoke.

'Telemachus, she has betrayed us all! She joined Stellos and his Novantae warriors.' Her face crumpled. 'She was with child. Stellos's child.'

'Where is Brigit now?' the senior soldier demanded. 'Is she with this Stellos and the children?'

Macha looked down in shame. 'She took one of our horses and rode west. She was in a state. I don't know where she went. I assume she has joined him,' she answered, her voice trailing off.

Lights exploded in Telemachus's head: find them, save them, kill Stellos, kill Brigit. As he raised his whip to spur on his horse, the senior soldier ordered him to stop.

Telemachus's head whipped around, fury and determination breaking from every part of him. 'NO!'

'Stop, I command you, in the name of the Prefect of the Cohort, Gaius Decimus Rufinus! I command you to stop.'

Sick with rage, Telemachus reined in his horse, glaring

with hatred at the senior soldier. Familial and military honour demanded obedience; they both knew it. 'We will return to the fort, to report to the Prefect. Forward!' As one, the patrol set off at a gallop, with Telemachus tossing a last look of fury at Macha, grim acceptance of human misery in her face.

The patrol galloped straight down the path, through the woods, through the meadows near the farm, through woods again and out on to the downward slope that ended at the Wall. As the Wall loomed out of the mist, they rode harder. The senior soldier brought them to the milecastle just east of Vercovicium, where they crossed into the south side of the Wall and continued riding to Vercovicium.

VERCOVICIUM SEALED

Upon hearing the news, Gaius immediately sealed the fort. No one could come or go without his express orders. Marcus was declared missing. Rumours circulated wildly around the fort. The Prefect ordered Quintus Valerius to assemble the main commanders in the Principia. These included Quintus, the *cornicularius*, the cavalry *optio*, the Tungrian *optio*, two of his *areani* and Grumio. The senior soldier of the patrol, the Nervian *decurion*, and Telemachus were there too. Gaius briefly informed the small group of the situation. The *cornicularius* assisted by pointing out salient points on the map, particularly to the two *optio*s, who would be leading their patrol.

The Prefect then specifically addressed his son:

'Telemachus, tell the group what you and Marcus planned for today.'

Pale, Telemachus told of the dawn appointment with Rhiannon, and how Marcus and Bran were to join them later in the morning. He explained how the plan was devised through notes carried by Brigit. Then he related how his father had, that morning, surprised him with the unexpected honour of accompanying the patrol to Hawk Ridge, meaning that he missed his meeting with Rhiannon.

Gaius broke in, looking at the senior soldier. 'Tell us what you learned from Macha, Brigit's cousin.'

When the soldier had finished speaking, there was a shifting among the group, some sitting, some standing, as they now realized the situation.

Gaius dismissed the senior soldier. 'We all know the region. The only place the raiders could hide is the forest below Hawk Ridge. We can use the ridge to our advantage.' He turned to Grumio. 'Grumio, find the three children. They will be held in a deer-skin tent probably, somewhere not very far from here, obviously north of the Wall. The camp could already be on the move. No one is as skilled as you for this job. Will you leave your retirement to find them?'

Grumio smiled drily, then raised his head to look at the Prefect. In silence, he nodded. Like magic the old man changed before their eyes. Telemachus knew what was happening from his times in the forest with the gentle gardener. A moment ago a worried, subservient *veteranus* had stood at the back of the room. All fear was now put behind him, gone. Grumio saluted Gaius, turned and left the room.

Gaius faced the group. 'Grumio is a brilliant scout. We spoke earlier and his advice is that the Novantae will have moved north-west, over Hawk Ridge. They'll know signals have been sent between the forts along the Wall and up to the forts in the northern outpost. Everyone will be on the lookout for them and they'll want to get into the great forest up in the north-west if they can. We'll lay an ambush for them on the Hawk Ridge.'

He then turned to the *optio*s. 'You will each command sixteen Tungrian infantry. Our *areani* will guide you to the ambush position. Afranus, pass through the Wall at the first milecastle east of Vercovicium. Carinus, you pass through the first milecastle west of Vercovicium. We will try to encircle them, meeting on the flat top of Hawk Ridge.'

He now addressed the last person in the room: 'Telemachus will join the twenty-four cavalry, under the *decurion*. They will be waiting in the woods. Meanwhile, our thirty-two infantry will have hidden beneath the lip of the plateau. They will surge up and engage the enemy, fighting in close formation – eight long and four deep. The main fighting will be done on foot, with spears and long slashing swords. After the infantry has the enemy in its grasp, the cavalry will strike like a hammer.

'Although our numbers will closely match theirs, we will have the clear advantage by our tactics, weapons and morale. Is that clear? The Ala Augusta will be riding from Cilurum, bringing two hundred cavalry to reinforce you and spread the net if we do not make contact. They've got ten miles further to come and it's uphill.' He allowed himself a grim smile. 'So be patient.'

The men nodded curtly, faces stern, ready.

'All but Telemachus dismissed.'

The two *areani*, the *cornicularius*, the two *optio*s and the *decurion* saluted, turned and left the room, leaving a petrified boy with the Prefect.

'Telemachus, after your mindless folly, which has endangered the lives of your brother, Bran and Rhiannon, it is now your chance to prove yourself.' He turned an impassive mask towards his son. Only his glittering eyes showed he was alive. 'When your mother heard this news, she screamed. Her face turned into the mask of tragedy and her waters broke. Our baby son slipped out, too easily, too quickly. I do not know if he will live. All this is on your head, Telemachus. Conduct yourself with dignity. Join the men you have trained so hard with. Slay the raiders. Should Grumio be successful, you will have been given a second chance – by the gods – to show you are a man.'

The cold afternoon sun shone into the Principia and on to them. Standing face to face, never had they so resembled each other: father and son, both ashen, the sinews on their necks like ropes, eyes unblinking. Telemachus saluted, turned and left the room.

HAWK RIDGE

In the freezing mist of the late, dark afternoon, thirty-two of the Tungrian infantry and twenty-four Nervii cavalry moved on to the upward-sweeping slope north of the Wall. To set the trap, the cavalry needed to reach the ridge before the raiders. They would hide and the infantry would close up on the ridge in a pincer movement. Telemachus rode with the cavalry up the ancient track, the same track upon which he and the patrol had travelled six hours earlier. Meanwhile, sixteen Tungrians, guided by an *areanus*, moved east half a mile along the Wall and sixteen, with their guide, moved west. Both forces crossed the Wall, headed north and began converging on the designated battle-ground. Silently and in single file, the two separate groups marched up the rolling plain.

Out of the dark came the screaming raiders, falling upon Afranus's sixteen men with ferocity. Immediately, the infantry formed themselves into a block – four deep, four across. On each side, they created a wall of shields, making it impossible for the raiders to isolate and cut down even one man. Although they were sixteen to the raiders' fifty, the raiders were disadvantaged by their horses, which could be gored by the soldiers' spears, the most deadly weapon in their arsenal. The raiders screamed as their legs were gashed. They screamed as their horses fell beneath them and then, tossing them to the ground, rolled over and crushed them. The slope was wet and slippery, first with winter snow, now with blood and viscera. The horses kept sliding sideways or down the slope. Many warriors leapt off their horses to throw themselves at the Roman formation, but they too were cut down by the killing machine. Stellos called for a retreat and the horsemen bolted up the slope to escape the murderous block of soldiers.

At the blast of a horn, the soldiers, still holding their formation, proceeded up the slope.

Alarmed at the cool efficiency of the soldiers' movements, Stellos knew before facing them again that his men had to regroup, to talk and plan. He thought to gain an advantage by retreating to the high plateau at the top of Hawk Ridge. But first he would take his men into the woods at the far north to give them time to gather, assess their losses, bandage the wounded and regain their courage, bragging about how many they would kill next time and how many shrunken heads would swing from their belts when they returned home. Possessing a skull meant possessing the dead man's power, knowledge and soul. None of his men yet possessed a single Roman skull.

Meanwhile, back in the raiders' tent, the three children sat in their wicker cages and through the tent opening saw the wiry guard warming himself by the fire, his back to the opening. A sudden movement made Bran twitch. There, at his cage's side, crouched Grumio. Marcus and Rhiannon saw Bran's movement and turned to see its cause.

Their surprise was compounded by Grumio's changed appearance. Bran looked into the face of the élite scout – detached, all business, no longer eager to please, no longer confused. Without pause Bran rapidly obeyed Grumio's silent commands. Grumio unleashed Bran's cage, indicated he should slip out and then unleashed the other two cages. He fixed his eyes on the three and waved his hand towards the south, towards the Wall. They understood. They were to get back on their own. Grumio glanced at the sentry and the boys nodded. He would take care of him and cover their flight. Rhiannon, he indicated, would travel with him. The boys agreed.

Rhiannon watched these commands. She let the two boys, accompanied by Nodens, slip out of the back of the tent and she followed Grumio, first taking their Novantae guard's long sword. Not fifty feet from the tent, she stopped him and whispered, 'Where is Telemachus?'

Grumio glared at her and turned away. She grabbed his sleeve and pulled his tunic right up to her face. 'Where is Telemachus?' she demanded, undaunted by his fierceness.

Grumio looked at her and saw she was an unknown quantity. He remembered her swordplay in the woods. He had to answer her or she would ask again loudly enough to alert the sentry.

'Back in the ambush. Hawk Ridge.'

'Take me to him – on horseback.'

Their eyes locked. He looked then for a way through the woods, around the blazing fire, to get to the raiders' stolen horses. He nodded, detached and professional again, and they moved. Within moments they had reached the horses. As Rhiannon jumped up to mount her horse, she saw a flash of blade and heard the crush of bone, even before she was aware of hands gripping her cloak to pull her down. In one fatal motion, Grumio had slashed the wiry sentry and mounted his horse. Settling herself and the sentry's long sword, she nodded to Grumio and they flew east through the woods towards Hawk Ridge.

Stellos felt his men were ready. He led them rapidly south-west, out of the cover of the woods, and gained the plateau. The raiders rapidly dismounted, giving their horses to the youngest warriors to hold. Feeling triumphant, the Novantae stood on top of the plateau and howled war-cries, shook their spears and banged their swords on their shields. They were a powerful force, their blood high for slaughter. Standing there ready, they bellowed for close combat, confident their great number would overwhelm the enemy.

Suddenly, thirty-two Tungrian infantry surged up, as if coming straight out of the earth. They swarmed on to the plateau, immediately forming themselves into a block, and began stabbing with their swords at the unprotected abdomens and armpits of the Britons. They swept forward and began killing mechanically, swinging tightly up and back, piercing skin and ripping entrails with each upward and downward movement.

Warriors eager to win fame demanded the auxiliaries' attention, roaring insults, thrusting their spears into the air, displaying their ferocity. Each warrior fought for his honour and few auxiliaries could match such bravery. Stellos saw this. But he saw also Death strike down his men.

He called for a retreat, yelling at those who still stood to run back to the horses. As they turned to obey, charging out of the western woods came the Nervii cavalry. Gaius's classic manoeuvre had worked. The hammer of the cavalry crashed down on the anvil formed by the infantry and crushed the raiders. Auxiliaries were before, behind and on top of the enemy. There was nowhere to run and no stopping the infantry's block of stabbing swords, now eight across. No stopping the long, chopping swords of the cavalry. Desperately engaged with the infantry, the raiders couldn't defend their backs from the simultaneous attack of the cavalry. Screams were cut short as the cavalry's long swords sliced the raiders' heads and thrust clean through their backs.

In the midst of twenty-four cavalry, unknown to Stellos, was the most deadly killer of all, Telemachus. His face expressed no emotion, only concentration and drive. These Britons had kidnapped his brother, the girl he loved and her brother. The shock had sent his mother into labour and may have killed his new-born brother.

Telemachus saw a raider, tall, powerfully built, running towards his horse, trying to escape. The raider's blue-white eyes locked on to Telemachus's and Telemachus knew that this was Stellos. He bore down upon him, oblivious to all other fighting. Stellos, seeing the murderous intent in Telemachus's eyes, hurled his sword as a spear into the horse's chest, felling him instantly. Pulling a dagger from under his cloak, Stellos, his arm upraised, charged towards Telemachus, who lay dazed. Suddenly, out of the dark mist,

Rhiannon appeared on horseback, red hair whipping in the wind. She swung the warrior's long sword, thudding it into Stellos's neck, half severing his head. Behind her rode Grumio, who hurled his javelin into Stellos's chest, so that the point stuck out from the middle of his back. Telemachus, having freed himself from beneath his horse, leapt on to Rhiannon's horse, behind her, and together they rode back into battle.

Now the combatants felt, then heard, the tread of hundreds of hooves. Looking up, they saw the Ala Augusta bearing down upon them. Two hundred men had ridden from Cilurnum to secure the victory. At battle's end, six auxiliaries had been killed, eight wounded, but of the fifty or more Novantae and Selgovae, none survived.

8 PAST AND PRESENT

THE CAVE

Bran, Marcus and Nodens ran, slipping, through the snow and wet woods. It was early afternoon, but the weak sun was already disappearing and what was left was obscured by dark, snow-filled clouds. The dank leaves and fir needles muffled sounds, so the running steps of the boys could hardly be heard. Only their breathing and pounding hearts seemed too loud to be ignored. Yet the warrior didn't follow them and, as Rhiannon hadn't followed them, they could only hope that Grumio had got her out successfully. The three ran and ran, through the woods, across fields and through more woods. The boys weren't sure where they were, but guessed somewhere north-west of Vercovicium. If they ran away from the weak sun and down to their right, they ought to come to the Wall, or at least see it soon.

Nodens was enjoying this part. Running with the boys through woods was his idea of perfection. He turned his head to bark joyfully but Marcus scowled at him to be quiet, so he hung his head a bit, all the while running at a clip. Hares darted left and right. There were squirrels too. He even smelled a fox. But there was no time for games today.

Today the game was running! He'd never seen the boys run so fast for so long. He wasn't tired, but he kept looking around at them to make sure they were keeping up.

Suddenly there was a cry and Bran disappeared. He had given a little wail of surprise and shot his hands up, while his body went down, as though he were jumping into a pool of water. Too late Marcus saw the hole, tried to stop himself, to catch hold of some bushes, but he succeeded only in twisting his fall so that he went down head-first. Nodens quickly doubled back and cocked his head sideways, looking down. No sound came from the hole.

In the darkness Marcus rubbed his head. He'd been knocked unconscious and had no idea how long he'd been asleep. Bran was gone! He looked wildly around and found himself in a broad, low-ceilinged tunnel dug into the ground and supported by lashed timbers. It sloped down deeper into the rocks. He had to find Bran. And where was Nodens? He would never leave me, Marcus wailed to himself in confusion and misery. They must have gone down this tunnel. He staggered to his feet and began awkwardly tottering down the dark slope. He stayed close to one side of the tunnel, to use it as a support. This must be a disused mine, he thought. It must have lots of tunnels. How will I know which one they've taken? His head throbbed and he felt sick with fear.

The light from the top of the hole helped him make out the way for a short while, but he could see darkness ahead. Just when he was about to despair, he noticed the flickering of a fire, deep down one of the tunnels. And he heard voices! Running his left hand along the wall, he quickened his pace, grimacing with each step as pain shot through his head. The ground surface was amazingly smooth. Perhaps worn, he thought. Once this might have been a rich mine.

As he drew closer, the fire seemed to brighten. Suddenly he was in a large space that was lit with the fire's golden glow. The fire was huge, its interlaced logs piled high in the centre of the room. He looked up, squinting against the brightness, to see the top of the fire or the roof of the room, but he could see no end to either. He was in a massive underground cave hewn out of rock. And sitting on the ground, cross-legged beside the fire, unbothered by the heat, sat Bran, happily chatting with two figures. One of them was barely visible, the other – Marcus could not believe his eyes – was Gurn.

Then Marcus made out the other figure: it was hideous, a witch, shaking and smiling, reeking of urine and mould and sweat. Her filthy hair lay matted on her head. Marcus could see lice moving around the hairline. She opened her mouth and he saw no teeth, only a wet, wobbly hole with a snake of a tongue rolling around in it. She was shaking and smiling at him. He looked more closely at her eyes and saw they were alert. He couldn't tell if they were mad or cruel. Gurn stood beside her, arms crossed over his chest. All three turned to look at Marcus.

'Greetings, Marcus,' the witch said, speaking Latin but with a toothless whistle. 'You fell through the earth to me,' she cackled while she continued to sway and shake. 'My own shooting star!' She laughed again. 'Or perhaps an earthworm?' She leaned close to him, as though to see more clearly whether or not he was a worm. Her stench made him gag. She hadn't heard, or ignored, the strangled sound and sat back again dreamily. 'Such a surprise. I remember years ago dropping in – though not so dramatically – on your Emperor Hadrian.' Marcus's eyes widened. 'He was sitting by the fire of a Briton, a woodcutter, in the wood-cutter's hut. I crept up, wet and hungry. I was given oaten loaves that had just been baked in the woodcutter's hearth.'

He couldn't take in what she was saying. He looked again at Gurn. He looked at Bran. Bran seemed completely at ease, yet here he was, under the ground, in an ancient cave and in the company of two spirits, perhaps even gods. Marcus found it hard to breathe and staggered backwards to a stone shelf, where he sat down, his head drooping. When he looked up, he hoped they might be gone, but they weren't. They had continued silently looking at him.

Gurn walked over to the fire and firmly planted his feet. He extended his arms and held his palms towards the fire, as though in blessing, Marcus thought. Marcus squinted to see in this great brightness. Gurn was praying. He slowly dropped his arms and turned towards Marcus.

Marcus frantically searched Bran's face for clues. Bran laughed and said, 'Don't worry, Marcus. These are our friends. This is Gurn, just as you suspected. And this,' Bran turned to look proudly at the crone beside him, 'is Queen Cartimandua, queen of the Brigantes.'

232

Marcus looked from one to another, but could say nothing.

Bran continued: 'I woke before you did from our fall and found Gurn standing beside me. I was terrified, but he smiled at me in a way that made me completely trust him.'

Marcus looked over at the muscular, tattooed figure outlined by the fire. He saw Gurn's thick gold torc, his spiked hair and his huge arms laced comfortably across his chest. He shook his head in disbelief.

'He asked me to follow him, to come to this ancient cave and meet the queen. Of course I came. Wouldn't you?'

Still, Marcus was too confounded to say anything.

Then Gurn spoke: 'We have brought you here, Marcus and Bran, for a purpose. We have watched Marcus since he came to our region and we have great hopes for him. We have watched Bran since he was little, since he was two years old –' he paused for a moment – 'and he too can serve us. I appeared to him in a dream when you visited the queen's fortifications. Do you remember, Bran?'

Bran looked amazed and nodded, while Marcus could only remain confused and scared. Gurn's voice was gravelly and quiet. His eyes were sad, but his face and figure were strong, imposing. Marcus knew he had terrific power. He was far too frightened to speak while Gurn's eyes held his.

Gurn brought his hands up to his face, as though in pain. As he did this, Marcus could see his muscles ripple and his gold torc glimmer in the fire's glow. The blue tattoos on Gurn's chest and upper arms that Marcus now could see were swirls, spirals, interlocking circles. They moved with his breathing. His moustache hid much of his face, but not his eyes, which held Marcus and seemed to pull him back into ancient times. How could his body be young and his eyes old? Marcus wondered.

Gurn looked deep into the fire and began to speak again: 'I am the Spirit of this Land, my region. I have many powers, Marcus. I have been here since life began. I do not have the power to make the crops grow, but I can help the farmers gather their seed, store it, plant it, harvest it. They cannot see me, unless I wish them to, but I am there, helping.' He rubbed his forehead and stared into the fire. 'I watched over my people when they first came here, thousands of years ago.'

Marcus looked scared and shifted on the stone bench. Still unable to believe his eyes, he looked again at Bran, who continued to sit calmly, right beside the spirits, right before the fire.

'I helped them live with the land, over thousands of years. I watched them survive. I taught them to make fire, to build stone huts, stone paths. I taught them to tame wild animals, tend cattle, sheep, goats, pigs, chickens and geese. They learned about the plough and how to yoke the oxen to pull it. Three thousand years ago, I saw them build their stone circles, over many generations, carefully placing each huge stone in its correct position, completing the circle. I watched as they built their massive burial mounds, stone chambers and corridors for the dead. They are a brave people, and dear to me. I have always been honoured by them. Then Marcus's people came.' Gurn arched his back and glared at the cave wall.

Marcus was terrified. He looked to Cartimandua for help. Her clothes were rags, putrid, torn. She had on layers of cloth, wool, linen, gauze, once of excellent quality – fit for a queen, he thought – though now stiff with mud. What help could she give?

Without moving a muscle, her eyes flickered on to him. He jumped. It was as though a shabti, an Egyptian figurine, had come alive. He couldn't bear to look into them, but he felt their intensity.

'Boy!' Her tone was urgent but, oddly, delivered as a whisper. 'I am the spirit of Queen Cartimandua. Bow and do me reverence,' she commanded.

Marcus heard her breathing and felt her eyes.

'Boy! I am not so old as the ancient Brigante. I have been a spirit nearly sixty years, but I too watch over my people.'

As she spoke, Marcus lifted his gaze and was horrified, mesmerized. She seemed to be changing shape! Her body was fluid, insubstantial, as though seen from above water. Her voice slid and turned, now a hoarse shriek, now honey-soothing. He feared her even more than he feared Gurn.

Extending her hand to him, silently she bade him approach. Feeling ill, Marcus half crawled, half shoved himself along until he knelt directly before her.

'When you Romans first came to me, I had to decide,' she began, her voice heaving now with old age. The skin on her face, when Marcus quickly glanced at her, was cracked and flaky. She raised her extended arm straight up and suddenly a beautiful goddess stood before him, too glorious to be captured in marble or stone. 'I chose the Roman Empire.' Her voice rose, commanding, demanding. 'Why did I do that, Marcus? Why did I welcome the Romans, Bran? My husband, Venutius, opposed the Romans. He led a civil war against me.' She leaned towards Bran and her voice became a low, terrible hiss. 'Was I a snake, Bran? Was I a traitor to the Brigantes?'

Marcus saw Bran had ceased his smiling, was solemn, listening carefully to the queen.

Silence in the cave. The beautiful queen dissolved into aged crone, with Gurn standing impassively at her side. No one spoke. Along the corridor from the cave, the boys could hear a rustling, a shuffling. Marcus's hair stood on end. Were there beasts in this cave, down the tunnels?

Gurn spoke. 'She was not a traitor. She saw –' he paused – 'the inevitable. She saw the Romans would conquer. By allying herself with them, she gave her people time to learn the Roman ways, to see the benefits, to accept *romanitas*. There was no choice, only a question of how and when. The days of the Brigantes, those days belong to another time, are gone forever.

'That is why I had to tell Stellos I would not help him.' His deep voice rumbled through the cave, chilling the boys. 'Stellos was once a good man.' He stopped speaking to look directly at each boy. 'But he would not accept that the Romans had changed our northern life.

'The Romans will leave us in three hundred years. The

Roman Empire will fall and, although many soldiers will return to their original homelands, many will stay.'

Marcus breathed heavily, hanging on every word. Bran was frowning.

'The Romans have shown us the power of a unified land. They've shown us what we can do when we are connected by language, law, roads and trade. Even if the north resists the Roman ways, the rest of the world has embraced and benefited from them. And even if the northern people insist on their independence, being as stubborn in their life on this stony soil as any heather or scrub pine, their lives will be harder than those of the Romanized peoples. Is this the legacy of a great leader to his people? No, Stellos was more wrong than right.

'I told him this. We quarrelled. He accused me of betraying his people as the queen had betrayed hers. He spoke wild and violent words. We heard him speak some to you too. He had changed, even while he fought to keep change out. In the end, he wanted to be the chief, but chief from a time before the Romans. It was impossible.'

Gurn's voice slipped like poured nectar into the boys' ears. They felt they were being hypnotized but had no power to stop him. 'Nearly two thousand years from now the same arguments will be heard – both in the north here and on the Western Isle. My ancient task is to protect my people and their land.'

'We show ourselves to those who will help us,' the queen then said. 'Bran, let me speak first to you.'

Bran stood before her and bowed his head.

'Bran, nearly eleven years ago you lost your father. You have missed him. You have needed his advice. Should you be like him, farming the land, offering your aid to the Romans?'

Bran had looked up at her the moment she spoke of his father, but now, Marcus could see, he was holding back tears.

'With your friend Marcus you have explored Vercovicium and seen the extraordinary strengths and benefits of the Roman Empire. You know how Coria has grown with the Empire's trade, and how my ancient fortifications have crumbled. Your mother speaks often to you and Rhiannon of how improved her life has been since the Romans came.'

She turned now to Gurn, bathing him in a sweet smile, and said, 'Gurn used to worry that the Roman roads were like a stone net thrown across his land, capturing it as if the hapless victim of a gladiator. This is not so.'

She turned back to Bran. 'My son, you were brave and sure confronting Stellos. You saw at once that Gurn was a friend. You have grown into yourself, Bran. You will become an impressive man, just right for the Roman auxiliary. Bran, you will join the army, travel across the world. Tell people about Britannia. Tell them your family's history and culture. Tell them about Gurn, the Spirit of the Land, and the people whose hard lives made this country. Tell them about me and how I negotiated with the Romans, gaining precious trade and time for the Brigantes. When you retire, return to help your people know more about the world and to feel they have a place in it. You are born in different times from your father. You will live to see the Roman Empire at its height.'

Bran stood straighter and taller during her speech. This was right, he thought. He turned to look proudly at Marcus, who now felt tears in his eyes.

'Marcus, rise,' the queen commanded. 'You too have worried about your future. You never realized that you have been travelling down your path the whole time.'

She smiled, but Marcus was not reassured. Just then, the odd rustling and shifting began again. Marcus looked down the far tunnel, from where the sounds were coming, and nearly fainted. Scores of spirits, scores and scores, all smiling at Marcus and Bran, were coming up the deep tunnel, into the room, towards him. They seem to know us, he thought, now mesmerized and baffled. Silently, they glided across the cave, then settled in a circle around the boys, not threatening, gently smiling. They were men, women, children, dressed in strange clothing, yet somehow vaguely familiar.

'You boys have met these Britons before, haven't you?' She smiled. 'Well, not quite met, but you have seen these people many times, Marcus, looking out of your cart and with Bran, across the fields? Bran knew, didn't you, that these spirits were friends. Marcus, at first you were afraid you were losing your mind, but no. You have the gift to see into the past, and to make the past real for the living. Write down everything you have seen. Preserve the record of Vercovicium, with its baths, hospital and barracks. But preserve too a record of the Brigantian ways. Write about

Modron's roundhouse and her settlement, about the wonderful metalwork of our people, our ancient fortifications and our gods. There is much to tell of these cultures. It takes a sympathetic heart to see a people, Marcus. Use your heart to help us. These spirits will always be there to guide you, they and hundreds of thousands more who wish their stories to be recorded and preserved. They live, like us, beneath the land. We, our lives, our stories, our values, underpin this land. Just look, and we will be there, beside you.'

Marcus understood her now. He, like Bran, knew that the future she described for him was exactly the future he wanted.

Bran raised his head and, looking at the two spirits, whispered, 'Is it always best to join the Empire?'

'No,' Gurn answered quietly. 'There are times to hold on to sovereignty. There is not one answer. You will be a soldier, Marcus will be a historian. Go out and see the world. See what you think.'

Gurn then extended his arms towards the fire, as if blessing it or taking in its magic through his fingers. The boys turned to look at the queen. Even as they watched, her body shimmered back and forth from goddess to crone. She seemed to be dissolving, but then she spoke again to them.

'Boys, take these things in memory of us. Bran, take this Brigantian brooch for your cloak, to hold it fast against the various weathers you will encounter.' She gave him a most beautiful circular piece of bronze and iron with coral inlay. 'For you, Marcus, we have this Brigantian bracelet. Its simplicity will remind you how easy it is to remember.' She placed into his hands an elegant circular bracelet of twisted, twined bronze wires. On its clasp was a small blue stone. The boys bowed their heads in thanks.

Marcus was intent on keeping his head down, of not looking up into the wonder of the spirits' faces, when he became aware of Nodens licking his face. He looked up and saw Bran lying beside him and the dog frantically leaping about. What? Where are Gurn and the queen? Where is the cave? he thought madly. But then Bran was sitting up and rubbing his head.

'Where are we, Marcus? What happened?' he asked.

'What happened!? You don't remember? You don't remember the spirits –'

Bran interrupted him. 'Of course I do! Where are they? What –'

At that moment, Nodens began barking and barking, causing the boys' hurt heads nearly to split. They heard voices and looked up to see the rim of the hole down which they'd fallen, and there was Telemachus! And Grumio! And Quintus!

'Here they are!' Telemachus called excitedly. 'We've found them, thanks to Nodens. Hello, old boy. Hello!'

FROM THIS DAY EVERMORE

Sometimes the late-winter sun can give just a bit of warmth, a whispered promise of long, hot days to come. So promised the winter sun that shone into the *tablinum* of the Praetorium the next morning. Bran and Marcus were arranged on day beds, with pillows, and little trays of sweet foods and warm drinks within easy reach. Gaius had just been speaking quietly in the corner with Telemachus and Rhiannon. Now everyone was gathered in a semicircle around the boys. Extraordinarily proud parents and adults smiled at them. Perhaps most eye-catching of all were Telemachus and Rhiannon, arms entwined, oblivious of the company. The only completely comfortable creature was Nodens, snoozing happily beneath Marcus's bed.

Claudia sat ensconced too in pillows, weak but glowing with relief and love. She was dazzled by the scene before her. So much had happened in one day! She had been terrified out of her mind when she learned Marcus and Modron's children had been kidnapped. Then the waters broke and the baby came, as though her very body had burst under the weight of the shock. Suddenly, home came Telemachus, Rhiannon and Grumio, then Marcus, Bran and Nodens. And the baby did live. Now, the next morning, exhausted as she was by everything, she was happier than she had ever been in her life. She smiled to remember how less than a year ago, approaching Vercovicium, Telemachus had complained about Claudius keeping his legions in Britannia. Britannia has been good to us, she thought. Telemachus has become a man. She looked over at him, entwined with Rhiannon, and a grin spread across her face. She turned now to Marcus and felt her heart swell to see his tired but brave young face. He too, she thought, has grown up and is now a much more serious boy than he was a year ago. Her gaze followed Gaius's movement as he walked to the centre of the assembly. She relaxed and was calm again, revelling in the certainty that, over the year, Gaius had been restored to them. He has shown himself an excellent father and – she hesitated – an attentive and loving husband. And now we have a wonderful baby, born of our new life in Britannia. It was good we came here, she thought, as she smiled and looked up at Gaius.

Gaius spoke. 'The gods have blessed us all.' He looked around the room. 'We must give thanks to Vesta, to Coventina, to Epona, to Brigantia, to Mithras –' Telemachus slightly blushed – 'to the *genii cucullati*, to Minerva and, most of all, to our father, Jupiter. We have all been blessed.

'I thank the gods on my own behalf. They have honoured me beyond any deserving. They have restored Marcus and his good friend, Bran. They have taken the boy Telemachus and returned the man you see before you. No Odysseus could be more proud of his son than I am of my Telemachus.'

The faces surrounding Gaius were bright with joy and wet tears.

'Modron, you are honoured as well by your children. Rhiannon has proved herself a true Brigante warrior in the highest tradition. Her battle-fury is now the stuff of legend. Your Bran did verbal battle with the warrior, Stellos, and then bravely endured with my boy the frightening fall into the disused mine.'

Modron beamed but was too relieved, proud and happy to speak.

'Grumio!' He smiled broadly at the fiercely proud *veteranus*, poised at attention before him. 'You, old friend —' and his voice softened — 'you saved the lives of all our children and we thank you.'

'Sir!' was all he said.

'And, if these were not reasons enough to celebrate, we also today announce the birth of a beautiful son, whom we have named Aelius, the family name of our great Emperor.

'Our only sorrow concerns Brigit, whom we loved as a member of our family. I brought her into our life, thinking she would make a perfect companion for my wife. I blame myself for not having thought more carefully through the difficulties of Brigit's situation.'

'No, no,' Claudia whispered, stung by her husband's self-accusations.

'She worked to do us harm but has been punished. The crimes were terrible, but so is the punishment of exile. Only the divine ones know what is appropriate. I leave that to them.'

'Sir,' Telemachus began, 'thank you for your praise of Rhiannon and myself —'

'I must speak for myself,' Rhiannon quietly interrupted. Suddenly shy, she dropped her chin, and her full fiery head caught and seemed to hold all the sun's rays.

The adults hid their smiles.

'Sir,' a chastised Telemachus began again, 'thank you. I needed to prove myself worthy of your good opinion and thank the gods I was given the chance. I too have an announcement. I would like to go soon to Rome, Father, to study under your brother, my uncle, to attain, if successful, the rank of procurator. A year ago, sir –' he looked directly at his father – 'I had only dreamed of wearing the *toga virilis*. Now I dream of following in my father's footsteps.'

Gaius nodded curtly, his face tight with emotion. Then, pulling himself together, he turned to the whole group, his face wreathed in smiles, and declared, 'It is with great pleasure that Claudia and I announce the betrothal of our son, Telemachus, and Rhiannon of the Brigantes. We have learned a great deal lately,' he said, abashed but happy, 'and would be deeply honoured by their union. As I understand their plans –' he shot a wry smile at the adults – 'Rhiannon will join him in two years' time, however far he has progressed in his career.'

'And I shall accept him,' Rhiannon quickly said. 'I had not thought I would marry a Roman of the military and equestrian ranks.' She looked around shyly at the welcoming faces, but she spoke with authority and dignity. 'I am inspired that his parents' marriage also combines Rome and the provinces. And I am deeply comforted to know that now, finally, I have crossed over and joined the same side as my father, who died for Rome, and my mother, who raised us under Rome's protection. I will always be a true daughter of the Brigantes and will not abandon our ancient ways. But now I embrace the Roman ways too.' She smiled into Telemachus's face.

Even Gaius felt a lump in his throat.

Marcus pulled himself up off the bed a little, clearly wanting to say something, but his father spoke first.

'Say nothing, Marcus and Bran. It is best if you sleep. What you have told us is the stuff of wild nightmares and is best left alone. You dreamed amazingly and imagined many wise speeches. Hold on to the wisdom, but let go of the fantasies. I shudder to think what might have happened if Nodens hadn't alerted us to your whereabouts.'

Marcus fell back, bewildered. Had it all been a dream? The bump on his head was real enough.

Upon hearing his name and the tone of praise, Nodens woke up and began banging his tail against the floor, a happy, expectant expression animating his bushy eyebrows and the whiskers along his long snout.

'Thank you for guarding our two boys here so well. You are a good dog. You saved them too, didn't you?' Gaius praised the big dog, stroking his back.

'Gaius, I think I must rest,' Claudia quietly interrupted.

'Yes, yes.' Gaius rose and resumed his place beside her and stood before the assembly. His face had grown serious. 'We thank the gods and we speak of future happiness. I am deeply fortunate that my wife and sons have joined me here at the edge of our Empire.'

Both sons smiled at their mother.

'And we are luckier still in our neighbours, who have come to mean so much to us.'

Here Modron, Bran and Rhiannon beamed.

'Our families are now as entangled as Rome and Britannia. Long may these entanglements last!'

Everyone cheered, nodding and laughing with delight. Then Gaius saw that Claudia was indeed worn out. He nodded to the slaves, who gently helped her gather her shawl and leave the room. Gaius smiled at Grumio, who was transformed, magically, into the Grumio of old. His shoulders dropped, his face creased into folds of worry and his eyes were again shy and uncertain. He was a *veteranus*, once a great scout, now a gardener for the Prefect's wife at Vercovicium. He turned and quietly left the room.

Modron looked over at her son and then at her daughter. She too smiled and quietly began to leave the room. Rhiannon called out to her mother to stop her and, running over to her, threw her arms about the heavy, unassuming woman and kissed her, causing Modron to laugh and protest. Telemachus grinned proudly and joined them as they left.

Finally, Gaius stood alone, facing the two younger boys.

'You've been through a lot and you've grown up, boys. Now rest,' he gently commanded, and left the room.

Nodens was asleep again under the chaise, his gentle breathing the only sound in the room. The boys didn't feel like talking, but turned, simultaneously, to gaze out of the window just level with their beds. The day had passed to late afternoon and it was cloudy, cold and beginning to rain. They could hear sheep bleating and the wind blowing. Wet, fresh grass and scents of fir trees wafted in to them. They could see the crows' untidy nests of twigs, precariously built into the branches, swaying with the wind. Two of the crows flew to the window-sill and peeked in. They saw the boys warm and safe while the wind blew rain about the folded hills and plains and woods.

Marcus looked over at his friend. He saw Bran frowning at the ceiling. Bran slid his eyes carefully over to Marcus, his head clearly still in great pain. The two said nothing for a moment.

'Bran, we're thinking the same thing now because we experienced the same thing only a few hours ago. We had the same story. We didn't make it up.'

Bran kept looking silently at Marcus. Marcus tried again.

'The queen said it was easy to remember, that the spirits that underpin this land are always about us, helping us, didn't she?' Something nagged at Marcus's memory. Easy to remember . . . easy to remember . . . He stretched out his right arm, pulling back the layers of clothes he was still wearing from outdoors and the blankets that had been heaped on top of him There was the twisted bronze bracelet with the blue stone on its clasp. Bran gasped and immediately slapped his chest just below the right shoulder. There was the circular bronze brooch pinned on to his tunic, under all the layers of outer clothes and blankets.

Both boys lay back on their beds and smiled. They glanced again at each other and grinned.

'Cock-a-doodle-do,' Marcus whispered.

'Cock-a-doodle-do,' Bran answered.

What a time it had been since they'd first yelled this out,

on the Wall, ages and ages ago. Off flew the two crows from the window-sill, raucously cawing and cawing as they soared into the winter sky.

ACKNOWLEDGEMENTS

I am grateful to The American School in London for sabbatical leave to write the novel and to Lt Col (Rtd) C. H. Jackman, RLC, for generously putting at my disposal his encyclopedic knowledge of Roman Britain and the history of Hadrian's Wall. Col Jackman read several drafts of *Power and Stone* and provided many shrewd suggestions, not least in the plotting of the battle scenes. An early draft of the manuscript was also read by Dr Lindsay Allason-Jones, Director of Museums, Museum of Antiquities, Newcastle, who saved me from numerous inaccuracies and improbabilities. I have tried throughout to couch my story in as accurate a historical context as possible. If errors remain they are my responsibility entirely.